O9-ABI-500

The old energy was still there.

One glance, one brushing touch of his fingers, told her that much. He'd come sneaking up behind her on purpose to catch her off guard.

"Hello, Sean," Robin said calmly. "I hear you're standing in for the best man. That was kind of you."

Her greeting was a let-down, but Sean played his role with equal grace. "Hi, Robin. I was happy to oblige," he said, and smiled . . . while the silence stretched. Finally, he blurted out, "Were you surprised that I'm included in the wedding party?"

She shrugged. "No."

A little flash of annoyance lit his eyes. She was playing it very cool. He decided to goad her. "You won't mind standing with me at the altar?" he taunted.

"Not under the circumstances," she said demurely. "As long as I'm only the bridesmaid, not the bride."

Sean felt the sting of her words but managed a laugh. "At last we're agreeing on something."

Dear Reader:

The spirit of the Silhouette Romance Homecoming Celebration lives on as each month we bring you six books by continuing stars!

And we have a galaxy of stars planned for 1988. In the coming months, we're publishing romances by many of your favorite authors such as Annette Broadrick, Sondra Stanford and Brittany Young. Beginning in January, Debbie Macomber has written a trilogy designed to cure any midwinter blues. And that's not all—during the summer, Diana Palmer presents her most engaging heroes and heroines in a trilogy that will be sure to capture your heart.

Your response to these authors and other authors of Silhouette Romances has served as a touchstone for us, and we're pleased to bring you more books with Silhouette's distinctive medley of charm, wit and—above all—romance.

I hope you enjoy this book and the many stories to come. Come home to romance—for always!

Sincerely,

Tara Hughes
Senior Editor
Silhouette Books

JOAN SMITH

If You
Love Me

Published by Silhouette Books New York
America's Publisher of Contemporary Romance

SILHOUETTE BOOKS
300 E. 42nd St., New York, N.Y. 10017

Copyright © 1988 by Joan Smith

All rights reserved, including the right to reproduce
this book or portions thereof in any form whatsoever.
For information address Silhouette Books,
300 E. 42nd St., New York, N.Y. 10017

ISBN: 0-373-08562-1

First Silhouette Books printing March 1988

All the characters in this book are fictitious. Any
resemblance to actual persons, living or dead, is
purely coincidental.

SILHOUETTE, SILHOUETTE ROMANCE and colophon
are registered trademarks of the publisher.

America's Publisher of Contemporary Romance

Printed in the U.S.A.

Books by Joan Smith

Silhouette Romance

Next Year's Blonde #234
Caprice #255
From Now On #269
Chance of a Lifetime #288
Best of Enemies #302
Trouble in Paradise #315
Future Perfect #325
Tender Takeover #343
The Yielding Art #354
The Infamous Madam X #430
Where There's a Will #452
Dear Corrie #546
If You Love Me #562

JOAN SMITH

has written many Regency romances, but likes working with the greater freedom of contemporaries. She also enjoys mysteries and Gothics, collects Japanese porcelain and is a passionate gardener. A native of Canada, she is the mother of three.

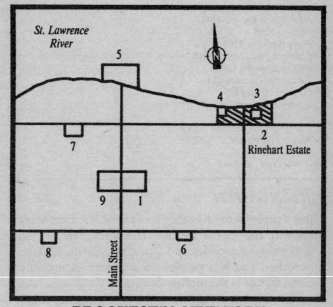

BROOKTOWN, NEW YORK
A fictitious town.

1. Halton's Hotel
2. Rinehart estate
3. Sean Blake's house
4. The cottage Robyn wanted
5. Skating Rink

6. St. George's Church, scene of wedding
7. Halton's house
8. Nora's house
9. City Hall

Chapter One

Robyn Halton pulled her compact car into the driveway and gave a sigh of relief. Home, safe and sound. The trip from Syracuse was only a hundred miles long, but between snow flurries and patches of ice, she was glad to have made it intact. Her brother, Ed, was getting married on the 30 December, and she didn't plan to miss that. She had rushed back to work the very day after Christmas and had scurried around reorganizing her schedule with obliging colleagues to be home a few days early to help out with the arrangements.

Robyn turned off the car's motor, got her suitcase from the trunk and struggled toward the house. The lights on the outdoor Christmas tree were still lighted. Reflections from them turned the newly fallen snow to a shimmering blanket of red and blue and green. Robyn shivered into her collar and hurried toward the door without really seeing the house, though a picture of it was in her mind's eye.

In her heart she still considered it home. It was this substantial stone house in Brooktown, New York that held warm memories of growing up in the midst of a happy family. They hadn't quarreled the way some brothers and sisters did. Robyn's brother was five years older than she, and her kid sister was nearly ten years younger. Maybe the space between them accounted for the relative peace.

The white door before her, set in the middle of an expanse of limestone, held a gigantic pinecone wreath. Above the door a graceful fanlight lent charm to the entrance.

When Robyn thought of home, she didn't picture it in winter. The lawn and English garden were her mother's pride and joy. She opened the door, already feeling good inside from thinking about her mother. She was glad to see the Christmas decorations were still up. Christmas had been such a scrambling hurry she felt cheated.

"Hi, I'm home!" she called, and listened.

Silence. Around her stretched an expanse of polished oak floor. Loops of imitation holly twined around the newel post and threaded up the stairs via the spindles. Through the archway into the living room, she had a glimpse of the Christmas tree.

"Is there anybody here?" she called.

From the kitchen she heard footsteps, not rushing to meet her, but proceeding at a leisurely pace. In a moment her sister appeared and Robyn saw why Jill hadn't answered. She wore a pair of headphones and carried a miniature tape player in her hand. Upon seeing Robyn she turned it off and removed the earphones.

"A new group, the Sandbaggers," Jill said. "Noreen gave it to me for Christmas. You're late."

"It's nice to see you, too." Robyn laughed and set down her suitcase to give Jill a hug.

Jill was at what used to be called the awkward age. When she'd started high school last September, she'd unbraided her hair, but she hadn't learned what to do with it yet. It hung in long, straight whips around her shoulders. Her nose and her brown eyes looked too big for her face. To add the final offense, she wore braces. Jill's usual jeans and sweater had been replaced by a dress for the party, and Robyn knew her sister felt out of place in such finery.

"Where is everybody?" Robyn asked.

"They're already at the hotel for the engagement party. Mom made me stay home to wait for you. What kept you so long?"

"I got held up at work. Why don't you run along to the hotel, sis? I'll be there as soon as I can, but I have to shower and change."

"Mom said to wait for you," Jill replied. "No hurry. The party'll be a drag, anyway." Robyn assumed this meant there wouldn't be any other teenagers there. "I have to wear this gross dress. I look like my math teacher, Miss O'Neill. A dragon."

Robyn silently agreed that the dress didn't suit Jill. It was peacock blue, and the cut was matronly. "It looks fine," she said.

Jill wrinkled her nose. "What are you wearing?" she asked.

Robyn glanced uncertainly at her suitcase. "I brought a few outfits home. I'll decide while I shower."

"I'll unpack for you," Jill offered. She loved to handle Robyn's beautiful clothes. In fact, she loved just to be with her sister, to look at her. Robyn was living proof that a gangly fourteen-year-old could grow into a beauty.

Robyn used to wear braces, too. Her hair had once hung in unattractive strands. Now it flowed like a smooth silken curtain, slightly curled at the ends. It was the same deep chestnut shade as Jill's. Their eyes were the same almond shape, too, except that Robyn's fitted her face better. Amber was the shade Jill called them, when she sat making faces in her mirror. One day her angular body would blossom into curves, and the braces would come off.

"Thanks, Jill. I guess we'd better hurry, huh?" Robyn said, and picked up her suitcase. They went upstairs together, talking.

"Are you coming home to stay?" Jill asked hopefully. "I know Eddie asked you to manage the office for him. Now that we've expanded the hotel, we need a full-time office manager, and you have experience."

"I'm thinking it over," Robyn said.

She'd been brooding over her decision since Ed had asked her to consider it. The Haltons had run a small hotel in Brooktown for as long as Robyn could remember. It was the reason she'd studied hotel management when she graduated from high school. She always assumed she'd come home and work in the family business. But that was before Sean, of course.

When her father died, the family had decided to add a wing onto the hotel with the insurance money. It had just been completed. Ed could use an experienced assistant to handle the increase in patrons. But could she be happy working in the same town as Sean Blake? Robyn firmly shoved Sean to the back of her mind.

"Eddie has a suite all picked out for you at the hotel," Jill hurried on eagerly. "In case you didn't want to move back home, I mean. He says you can decorate it for yourself, and he'll pay you whatever you're making at the hotel in Syracuse."

"It's a tempting offer," Robyn admitted.

She considered the offer as she took a quick shower. It would be nice to be back in Brooktown, where she'd grown up. Her family and best friends were all here. She loved the city that sprawled along the southern bank of the Saint Lawrence River. It was like a holiday resort in summer, with the yacht club practically on their doorstep.

She missed the water when she was in Syracuse. What people in other towns called rivers looked like streams to her. The Saint Lawrence, dotted with the famous Thousand Islands, was a majestic, flowing torrent of green a mile wide. Brooktown was surely one of the most beautiful cities in America.

Working for a big hotel chain wasn't as satisfying as working for yourself. The Halton Hotel would be hers and Eddie's and Jill's one day. She'd have a say in how it was run. It could be a real challenge. Brooktown wasn't a large city, but it was growing by leaps and bounds.

Really there was nothing stopping her except lethargy. Certainly not Sean Blake. Why should she let *him* rule her life? He was nothing to her now but a memory. A nagging, rather annoying three-year-old memory filed under "unfinished business," and occasionally drawn out for consideration. She still owed him one.

Had she done the right thing by leaving town after they broke up? It all had happened so fast. She'd just come back from college that summer and started to work for her father. Sean hadn't been working long, either. His construction company was just getting off the ground. They were crazy to even think of getting married, but like two young fools in love, they'd gone ahead and gotten engaged.

Fortunately her parents liked Sean and hadn't objected to an early wedding. In fact, they were willing to help out financially. Everything would have been fine if Sean had accepted that very attractive offer from Mr. Britten as assistant manager of Britten Construction Company, with a salary that was twice what he was managing to make himself.

But no, not Sean. He always had to do things his own way. He wanted to work for himself, to be his own boss. He had to have everything his way. He was the one who had to choose where they'd live. Eventually he'd wanted to build a house, but they'd have meanwhile lived in a cramped little apartment.

Robyn had found the perfect starter house for them. It was a sweet little brick cottage on the river. Her father had offered them the down payment as a wedding present, and they could have afforded the mortgage payments if Sean had taken the job with Britten. The cottage was the guest house of the Rinehart estate, which was being broken up at that time.

The four acres of land had been severed into smaller lots. That cottage she'd wanted Sean to buy must be worth a fortune now. Waterfront property had sky-rocketed in price.

Here she was thinking of Sean Blake again, Robyn noticed with a frown of distaste. It was hard to forget a man who had jilted you in public. Of course she'd jilted him in private first. Given back the little engagement ring of emerald and diamond chips that had belonged to his mother. Never wanted to see him again, the whole foolish bit. Wouldn't answer the phone, wouldn't see him. Lord, she'd been so childish.

But not as bad as Sean. It wasn't the man's place to send the retraction in to the newspaper. "Mr. Sean Blake wishes to announce the termination of his engagement to Miss Robyn Halton." She still squirmed to remember it. She had expected that Sean would somehow have overcome her resistance and patched things up. Instead he had put that insulting notice in the newspaper, for all her friends to laugh at and smirk over.

Robyn's blood still ran hot to remember it. She hadn't seen any other alternative but to leave town. Getting a job at a hotel in Syracuse had been easy with her dad's connections and her training. Why was she raking all this up in her mind again?

It was these visits home that always set her off. Not that she saw Sean very often, but it seemed she couldn't drive through town without seeing one of his signs, posted in front of some building he'd got the contract for. Renovations by Blake Construction, Sean Blake, Prop. Sean specialized in authentic restorations of landmark architecture, but did some new buildings, such as the church, too.

Ed said he was building the new executive houses in the suburbs. You didn't see any Britten signs these days. Sean had bought Mr. Britten out. Ed had even given Sean the contract to expand the Halton Hotel.

"His ideas are so bright and original," Ed explained when she objected to using Sean. "And his tender is the lowest price, too. Quality and price—how can we accept any other bid?" he asked reasonably.

Robyn didn't want to appear unreasonable, so she went along with Ed's decision. She hadn't come home during the whole time the construction was taking place. Was that an accident or a subconscious reluctance to confront Sean? Of course she came home for Christmas, and she admitted Sean had done a wonderful job on the expansion. He hadn't touched the original facade, but the wing added at the back was totally modern. Sean had used glass and steel, inset with reclaimed brick and some black wrought-iron features, to harmonize with the appearance of the original building.

It was during the Christmas visit that Ed and Noreen Crawley finalized their wedding plans. Robyn had thought they'd have a spring wedding, but Ed felt the quiet spell after Christmas was a more convenient time. Mr. Spence could manage the hotel for two weeks. Spring and summer were the busiest seasons at a resort area hotel. The first two weeks of January were when Noreen could take her holidays from the hospital where she nursed. So Saturday, December 30 was the date chosen.

It was going to be a small but formal wedding. The bride would wear white satin. Robyn, the senior bridesmaid, would wear an emerald-green gown, and Jill would wear gold. Noreen's brother Mike was going to be the best man. All these details had been decided and were revealed to Robyn over the short Christmas holiday. With so many arrangements to be looked into, it had hardly seemed like Christmas at all, so Robyn was glad to be having this second Christmas season visit.

She stepped out of the shower and wrapped herself in a fluffy white towel to redo her face for the party. The moisture in the room had curled her hair in tendrils around her forehead. She brushed it out loose and began applying her makeup. Her almond-shaped, slightly slanted eyes were her best feature, and she spent most of her time on them.

"Whoever heard of a woman with golden eyes?" Sean had said. A wistful smile curved her lips. He did say the prettiest things. His Irish ancestry must have given him his silver tongue. Her eyes weren't golden at all. They were light brown. She applied a touch of bronze eye shadow and drew a fine line below her lashes. Winter had robbed her face of color, so she smoothed on a little rouge and carefully applied lipstick.

"I wish I could look like that," Jill said forlornly. "These darned braces make bumps in my lips." They also caused a slight lisping effect when she spoke.

"Don't wish your life away," Robyn said automatically. It was what her mother used to say to her. "It'll come with age."

"What are you going to wear? Mom's wearing her new blue Christmas dress."

"Then I'll wear my new Christmas dress, too," Robyn decided, and Jill dashed to the closet to get it.

It was a dark green crocheted dress, perfectly plain. The neckline was high and round, the sleeves long, the skirt straight. It wasn't till the dress was on and accessorized that its style became apparent. It clung loosely to the enticing curves of Robyn's body, highlighting her breasts and small waist without exaggerating them.

A bright scarf and a big gold pin brought the dress to life. It could look like a dozen different outfits, depending on what Robyn wore with it. High-heeled green alligator pumps were the final touch. Jill noticed how they accentuated Robyn's thin ankles. She frowned at her own medium heels. Stupid black-patent shoes with a ribbon bow. Miss O'Neill had a pair just like them.

The sisters talked as Robyn got dressed. "Did Ed and Noreen get the reservations for the Bahamas?" Robyn asked.

"Yes, and they're having the wedding lunch in the new dining room at our hotel. We're having champagne," Jill added proudly.

"We?"

"Ed said I can have a glass for the toast. On Friday there's a dress rehearsal at church. Noreen's mother is having a party after at her house."

"That just leaves tomorrow for me to buy them a present. I wonder what they'd like."

"Noreen wants a funny-looking lamp with a big white base. It looks like a giant golf ball wearing a poke bonnet. It's at Peterson's Furniture Store. I think it's ugly."

"She likes modern," Robyn mentioned, and glanced at her sister in the mirror as she put the final touches on her hair.

She noticed Jill was biting her underlip. Experience had taught her that this spelled trouble. When Jill was trying to look innocent, she bit her lip.

"Is there something you want to tell me, Jill?" she asked.

Jill's almond eyes widened in an innocent gaze. "What do you mean?" she said, and began twisting the end of her hair between her fingers, another dead giveaway.

"You look—sneaky," Robyn said for lack of a better word.

"I haven't done anything."

"Then you're planning to." Robyn smiled and picked up her purse. "If you intend to sample the wine tonight, sis, I suggest you go very easy. Dilute it with soda water."

"I don't like wine. It tastes grody. I prefer beer, like Sean."

A quiver like an electric shock went through Robyn at hearing Sean's name. Jill had probably seen quite a bit of him when the hotel was being expanded. They'd always got along well, considering the disparity in their ages. Sean took the trouble to get to know people he liked. Robyn hesitated a minute before speaking. "I wouldn't take Sean as my guide."

"Why not?" Jill asked quickly. "Why don't you like him anymore, Robyn? I think he's the nicest boyfriend you ever had."

"Certainly the nicest one who ever jilted me in public," Robyn said with an angry look at her sister. "You know the story."

"You gave him back the ring first. Lots of people announce the end of their engagement."

"Lots of women!"

"Did you think he was going to back down and take the job with Britten?"

"Have you seen my white scarf, Jill?" Robyn asked, ignoring the question entirely. Of course that was exactly what she had thought.

Jill stared suspiciously. In the mirror she caught the angry spark in Robyn's eyes. "It's right under your coat," she said, and pulled it out.

"You heard about Noreen's brother?" Jill asked with exaggerated nonchalance.

"What do you mean?"

"Mike broke his leg skiing yesterday."

"Oh, Lord!" Robyn exclaimed. "That's too bad. He'll look awkward at the wedding."

"He can't be the best man. It was a compound fracture. He's in traction at the hospital."

"I'm sorry to hear it. Poor Mike was always accident-prone. Who's going to take his place?"

"Didn't they tell you?" Jill's clear amber eyes stared like an odalisque's from the bed. "Sean Blake's going to replace him. Ed always liked Sean. They've become good friends since Sean did the hotel."

Jill watched with the keenest interest as her sister's face blanched to white, with two patches of pink where she'd applied her rouge. Robyn could try to act unconcerned as much as she wanted to; Jill knew she still loved Sean. He and Rob were perfect for each other. But Jill had to make them see it. "You needn't worry he'll pester you again," she added matter-of-factly.

"I'm not worried," Robyn exclaimed. "I know how to handle him."

"Oh, you won't have to handle him. He's engaged now."

Robyn's face looked for a minute as if it had turned to stone. Jill felt a terrible twinge of guilt. It was all her fault! She had unwittingly made Sean get engaged to a woman he couldn't possibly love, since he had to love Robyn.

Robyn turned away and asked in a voice that tried to sound casual and only succeeded in revealing her rampant interest, "Who's he marrying? Anyone I know?"

"Meggie Britten. He took over their family construction company when Mr. Britten retired, you know. Then he started going out with Meggie. I guess he couldn't help falling in love with her, she's so beautiful." A cagey light glowed in Jill's amber eyes. "Don't you think she's awfully pretty, Robyn?" Personally Jill thought she had all the appeal of a sweet and gooey marshmallow sundae.

"Yes, of course, if you like that type." If you happened to like blond and gorgeous and rich. She could hardly believe it. Sean and Meg Britten.

Yet as Robyn considered it, she thought Meg would make the perfect wife for an overbearing man like Sean. She'd never been known to raise her dulcet voice in public. She'd smile and tell him he was perfect. That was Robyn's opinion of her, though Meg had never been one of her set. Meg had no career ambitions, either, as far as Robyn knew. "Daddy" wanted her to stay home, so she'd stayed home. No doubt Sean would want her to stay home and take care of him, too. At least he hadn't suggested that to Robyn!

"Yeah, she's kind of wimpy," Jill admitted. "I always thought you'd suit Sean better. I was sure you two would get together again."

"No way," Robyn said firmly. She turned away and picked up her coat. "I'm all set. Shall we go?"

"We'd better. We're late already."

As Robyn put on her fur-collared coat, she said reluctantly, "I suppose Sean and Meg will be at the party tonight?"

"Oh course. Gee, I love that coat, Rob. That big fur collar and full skirt make you look like a Russian princess."

"Thanks," Robyn said just before her jaw clenched mutinously. Did she really *have* to go to this party? She was dog tired after the drive home.

Jill watched, fascinated. "Why did you and Sean break up, Rob? I was just a kid at the time. I know I never heard the real story."

"It's no secret. Sean's company wasn't doing very well. He was offered an excellent job with Britten. He refused to take it."

"But why should you break up with him over that?" Jill persisted. "I wouldn't want a man I could push under my thumb. It's his life."

Robyn felt a familiar stab of guilt. She'd often had this discussion with herself. Was she right to have insisted? She repeated the well-rehearsed rationalization. "When two people are married, it's *their* life. He didn't even consult with me. He just turned the offer down flat. He knew I wanted that cottage on the river, too. Even if he'd worked for Britten for a couple of years, he could have paid Dad back, since he wouldn't take the down payment for a wedding present. He wasn't willing to make *any* compromises.''

Robyn noticed she was speaking rapidly, harshly. They were still there—the old anger, the pinching hurt. How little it took to bring them boiling to the surface. She'd thought she was over Sean. If it weren't for that grudge she had to pay off, she'd have forgotten him years ago.

Why had he chosen that humiliating way to write finis to it all? She'd been so sure Sean would agree to her demands, and then to open the newspaper and see the announcement. Her hand trembled as she flung open the door and hurried downstairs, out the door and toward her car.

Jill scampered after her, still gabbing. ''You should have stuck around,'' Jill said. ''You could have changed his mind. How did you think you were going to change his mind by running away?''

''I wasn't trying to change his mind. I know a hopeless case when I see it. Dad didn't need me to help with the hotel then. Ed had just joined him. I decided to get some experience in a bigger hotel in the city.''

''Sean said you ran away.''

''When did he say that?'' Robyn demanded.

Jill began biting her underlip. ''I dunno, exactly. He used to talk to me when I was hanging around the hotel. I asked him what happened one day.''

Robyn felt choked with rage. ''In future, I'd thank you not to discuss me with Sean Blake.''

Jill shrugged her shoulder. "Careful or you'll burst a blood vessel. There's no reason to discuss it now, is there? He's getting married to Meg. It's all over. Personally I think you made a terrible mistake. But I guess you must love Jeff Perkins. What's he like?"

"He's reasonable," Robyn said, and turned the key in the ignition.

She didn't spend a minute thinking about Jeff Perkins. He was already history. She'd been seeing him when she was home for Christmas, but only as a casual friend. Since everybody had asked her who she was seeing, she'd spoken about Jeff. It was Sean she thought of as she drove along the snow-clad roads, peering through her frosty windshield for oncoming traffic.

Stubborn, uncompromising, maddening Sean Blake. Handsome Sean Blake, with his blue Irish eyes that made star sapphires look dull. And his Irish temper that meant he wasn't happy until he had a fight brewing. But what marvelous fights they had had, and what marvelous reconciliations. She could never stay angry with him for long. He was just too irresistible.

Sean brought new meaning to the trite phrase "tall, dark and handsome." He was six feet and two inches of pure kinetic energy. The kind of man who could never sit still. He had to be doing. His hair wasn't just dark. It wasn't just black. It had the iridescent sheen of a raven's wing. Glints of blue shone in its mink-soft depths under artificial light. In the full sun, it mirrored the colors of the rainbow. His complexion was ruddy from his outdoor work. And those eyes! They seemed literally to sparkle when he was excited or when they were alone, talking of their love.

Now he was engaged to Meg. Robyn felt an angry heat grow in her breast. How could she face everybody at this darned party? How could she walk in with a smile on her face and congratulate Sean and Meg on their engagement? If she came back to Brooktown to work, she'd have to see them frequently. But she was being silly. Time heals all wounds. She hadn't thought of Sean for ages.

She wouldn't let him do it again. He was the reason she'd left Brooktown in the first place, but he wouldn't make it impossible for her to come back. The nerve of him, telling Jill she'd run away! She hadn't run away—had she? Well, maybe she'd walked rather quickly. Her pride didn't relish the smirks and smiles of her so-called friends, and that was his fault.

The man didn't have a reasonable bone in his body. She was well rid of him. As if to mock her, she passed a large sign in front of the fine old Almquist house. It was a landmark in Brooktown. It had been damaged by fire, and Sean was restoring it to its former glory. Renovations by Blake Construction, Sean Blake Prop. The sign seemed to be saying this had become Sean Blake's town. She was no longer welcome.

Then she turned the corner, and the Halton Hotel came into view. She felt proprietary and proud of its elegant appearance. It looked like a discreet old dowager, with its quaint torch lamps decorating the old brick facade, and the grilled glass doors set in a deep recess. European, the tourists called it, because it was low-key and catered to its clients. What they meant, she thought, was old-world charm.

Dammit, she wanted to come back to her dad's hotel. This was her town, too. Her family had lived here for a century before Sean Blake moved in. He hadn't even gone to school here; he was from Boston. She'd come back if she wanted to.

Maybe Sean's getting married was a good thing. She could write finis to that file labeled "unfinished business" and get on with her life. One small corner of her heart rankled that she hadn't managed to even the score, but it was time to outgrow that childish wish for revenge.

"We're here," she said, and pulled into a parking lot across the street.

Jill looked out the window. "I see Sean's here, too," Jill mentioned with a glinting glance at her sister. "That's his car."

Robyn looked out the window and saw a dark Porsche. He was doing well! He used to drive an old paneled van when she went with him. "There's a better parking spot ahead," she said, and pulled forward. "Now I won't have to back out," she explained to Jill, who gave her a very adult and knowing look.

"Sure, Rob. Sure."

Chapter Two

Robyn and Jill passed through the lobby of the hotel to the new addition, where the party was being held. Robyn grudgingly admired how ingeniously Sean had blended the old and the new. The glass-covered walkway would flood the passage with light by day. Reclaimed brick with its patina of discoloration removed the air of glaring newness. Antique plant stands held pots of tumbling ivy and fern, turning the area into a conservatory, lighted from above and below.

They checked their coats and entered the crowded room. This particular space had been designed for smaller catered affairs and business meetings, but even here Sean's attention to detail was apparent. Soft, indirect lighting cast a welcoming glow on the peach-colored draperies that covered one wall. Paneled oak beams formed the other walls, punctuated at intervals with old-fashioned bracket lamps that mimicked gas-light. The overall effect was intimate.

Robyn stood a moment at the door, surveying the throng. To the casual observer, it seemed she was looking for the prospective bride and bridegroom. Actually she spotted Ed and Noreen from the doorway. It was Sean Blake that she was looking for. Not that she planned to join him. She meant to stay as far away from him as possible.

She heard, from the midst of the crowd, his telltale laugh, and something inside her tightened. "The lilt of Irish laughter," her mother used to say with a fond smile when she heard it. Infectious, bubbling over with enthusiasm and high spirits, a little loud, but no one ever minded that. "A big man should have a big voice," her mom had said.

Every detail of that romance was etched sharply in Robyn's mind. All it took was the sound of his voice to wash away the veneer of indifference. Then she remembered the hot Irish temper that formed the other side of Sean's nature—the side that had sent in that retraction. Did he ever get angry with Meg Britten, she wondered. Probably not. Meg looked as if she'd break if anyone shouted at her.

Jill pulled at her sleeve. "There they are," she said, and began walking toward Ed and Noreen.

Robyn followed, wearing a smile of greeting. She was welcomed amid a shower of exclamations and questions. "Did you run into the storm?" "Were the roads very bad?"

From her mother she received a hurried hug. "Have you had any dinner? You must be starved!"

At fifty-eight Mrs. Halton was still attractive. The gray wisps at her temples added dignity to her appearance. Robyn hoped she'd age as well. The almond eyes and chestnut hair were similar. Ed had inherited his father's blue eyes and Roman nose.

Robyn soon redirected the conversation to the more important couple. Noreen looked radiant. She wasn't beautiful, but she had what was more important: charm. She was only five feet tall, her red curls were hopelessly frizzy, and her usually pale complexion was altered with inexpertly applied rouge, but her green eyes glowed with love. Ed Halton, at six feet, had to bend down to put his arm around her.

The ever-moving crowd moved again, and Noreen drew Robyn aside. "Come on, we'll get you a plate of hors d'oeuvres. We don't want you passing out from hunger. The tiger shrimp is fantastic. Your chef does them in a spicy sauce that's out of this world. I have about a million things to discuss with you, but first—" She stopped and gave Robyn a doubtful look. "Do you mind very much about Sean acting as our best man? We were desperate when that klutz of a Mike ended up in the hospital."

"Don't be silly. I don't mind in the least," Robyn lied firmly. The echo of that denial sounded false, even to herself.

Noreen gave her a doubting look that soon settled to relief and led her to the serving table. "I didn't think you were still angry at him."

Apparently she'd convinced Noreen, who immediately went on to talk about other things. Had she seen her bridesmaid gown, and did she think it was too dark? She'd have to try on the headdress. The woman had made the bands so tight they might cause a headache. Robyn listened, nodding at the proper intervals, but it took most of her concentration and all of her willpower to keep from looking at Sean.

It was a relief when Ed came and reclaimed his fiancée. It left Robyn free to think. She stood at the serving table with her back to the room, selecting food. She was ravenous from the long trip. The trays of cold meats and shrimp and cheese looked appetizing.

Other people were filling plates, too. As Robyn didn't recognize them, a smile was all that was required of her. They must be Noreen's relatives from out of town. She reached for a stick of celery, and her fingers collided with a man's hand.

"Sorry," she said automatically, and glanced up. A wrenching spasm seized her when she found herself gazing into Sean Blake's infamous blue eyes. Her whole body froze, as if they were playing statues. She hadn't seen him for six months. She hadn't actually felt his touch for three years. It was still an electrifying experience. The old energy was still there. One glance, one brushing touch of his fingers told her that much. She felt devastated. And Sean was enjoying her confusion. She recognized that glinting triumph that sparked from his eyes. He'd come sneaking up behind her on purpose to catch her off guard.

Robyn was very proud of herself. She didn't gasp or blush or turn white when she met Sean's sardonic gaze. She had mentally braced herself for the confrontation, and other than that instant of freezing, she carried it off well.

"Hello, Sean," she said calmly. "I hear you're standing in for the best man. That was kind of you."

It was a letdown that Sean played his role with equal grace. "Hi, Robyn. I was happy to oblige," he said, and smiled at her blandly while the silence stretched.

He didn't seem to feel anything, not a thing. No shame, no remorse, nothing. She might as well be a total stranger. The silence stretched uncomfortably as the memories washed over her. Sean hadn't changed much. He still carried his spectacular good looks with an air of nonchalance. Coal-black hair swept back from a high brow. His nose, large and sculptured, lent an air of masculine authority to his face. His rugged jaw emphasized it. Was there just an edge of antagonism in the set of that firm jaw? She must be imagining it. His gaze didn't flicker.

Finally he broke the silence. "Were you surprised that I'm included in the wedding party?" he asked, studying her with mild curiosity.

She chose to evade the question by subtly shifting its meaning. "It comes as no surprise that Mike incapacitated himself," she replied. "He wore an arm sling to his own wedding, as I recall."

"That must have thrown an interesting light on the honeymoon." He smiled. "But I meant were you surprised that Ed chose me to replace him?"

She shrugged. "No."

A little flash of annoyance lighted his eyes. She was playing it very cool. Sean decided to goad her. "You won't mind standing with me at the altar, then?" he taunted.

"Not under the circumstances," she said demurely. "As long as I'm only the bridesmaid, not the bride."

Sean felt the sting of her words but managed a laugh. "At last we're agreeing on something. I didn't know, when Ed asked me, that you were going to be the bridesmaid."

"I'm his sister and Noreen's best friend. Who else would they have? Anyway, would it have mattered?" she asked.

"Not to me!"

"Then there's no problem, is there?"

"I just didn't want you to think I was—" Sean came to an abrupt halt. He couldn't think of any possible way of ending that sentence without sounding either idiotic or overbearing. *I didn't want you to think I was chasing you,* was what he meant. How could an engaged man be chasing an engaged woman? And why wasn't she wearing her engagement ring? It was the first thing he'd noticed when their hands touched at the celery tray.

Robyn listened, eyebrows lifted in amused interest. When she decided he was finished, she gave a mocking smile. "Don't worry, Sean. I don't think about you at all."

"The feeling is mutual," he said, mimicking her expression.

"You mean the *lack* of feeling, surely."

Despite Sean's easy attitude, Robyn began to feel the air was charged with feeling, all of it negative.

Sean examined the table and said, without looking at her, "I'm glad to see you're being so reasonable.

There's no reason we can't act like adults about this thing. It'll only be for a few days.''

"Yes, I'm surprised you're making such a big deal of it,'' Robyn replied. She expected to see some reaction to that thrust. Sean popped an olive into his mouth and chewed.

"Big deal? All I said was I hoped you weren't upset that I'm included in the wedding party.''

"I'm not,'' she replied, and gave a careless smile. "Do you want to try some of this shrimp? Noreen recommends it highly.''

Sean held his plate and she scooped some shrimp onto it. "Did you have a good Christmas?'' he asked.

"It was a mad rush, with Ed and Noreen getting ready for the wedding. I don't see why they're rushing things so.''

"Best to get on with it while they're in the mood,'' Sean said, and immediately realized he had strayed into troubled waters. The knowledge of their own broken engagement stretched before him like a field of land mines.

Robyn decided to ignore Sean's comment. "They've already been engaged for two years. That's why we were all surprised at the hasty wedding.''

A glint of blue brilliance flashed behind Sean's long lashes. "I'm all for hasty weddings myself. If people wait too long, something might happen to break the spell.''

Robyn felt her insides squeeze into a knot and made a supreme effort to hide her feelings. "You and Meg will be darting to the altar at top speed, I take it?''

"We'd have been there before now if it weren't for the play Meg's involved in. She's got the lead in the Brooktown Dramatic Society's new production."

"And you're reduced to playing second fiddle. That does surprise me." She spoke in a pleasant voice. The words carried their own sting.

"I happen to be very busy myself. I'm restoring the old town hall."

"I noticed the sign when I was home at Christmas."

"Isn't Jeff with you? I thought we might get to meet him," Sean said.

"Jeff?" she asked, surprised. "No, he's not coming. Where did you get that idea? He doesn't know Ed or Noreen." She wondered how Sean even knew about Jeff. But she wasn't sorry to let him think there was an important man in her life. "Jeff's very busy, too," she added. "He's a corporate lawyer."

"One of the Ivy League crew, I expect?"

Sean had always been tender about his lack of a university education. Robyn could never figure out why this should bother him, especially now that he was so successful. She didn't intend to dwell on the matter.

"He's a Westerner, actually." After a little pause, Robyn tightened her control and said brightly, "I haven't had an opportunity to congratulate you on your engagement, Sean. Jill mentioned it on our way here tonight. All the best. I'm sure you and Meg will be very happy."

She looked, expecting to see his triumphant smile. Sean was examining her intently. "Weddings go in threes. I imagine you'll be the next one to make your announcement," he said with a questioning look.

"You'll read the notice in the papers when it happens—if you're interested," she replied with a little emphasis on the words "notice in the papers." That should get some reaction.

Sean gave her a wary look. "If that's a dig about the announcement I—"

"Let sleeping dogs lie, Sean," she suggested.

He relaxed visibly. "I'm always interested in old friends," he assured her.

Sean thought he gave just the right, careless touch to that answer. The meeting hadn't gone too badly. He hadn't thought it would be quite this upsetting, seeing Robyn again. She could always get under his skin. And in the past he'd done a pretty good job of getting under hers, too. They were too much alike, that was half the trouble. Both too hotheaded, but tonight it was her calmness that infuriated him.

"Hey, I'm not that old!" she laughed lightly.

He'd try a sharper thrust. "A quarter of a century, isn't it?" he taunted.

"Close, but no cigar. I'm twenty-four," she replied, unfazed. *As if you didn't know!* His mother's engagement ring, given on her twenty-first birthday—he couldn't have forgotten that!

"It's not much, but it's the thought that counts," he had said. "One day I'll give you a diamond as big as the Ritz." But he'd given it to Meg Britten instead. And where was Meg, anyway?

Robyn looked around and spotted Meg in the doorway. She was staring at Robyn and Sean from across the room, with a pensive, assessing expression on her beautiful face. Suddenly every other woman in the room looked plain. Meg had a small, dainty face. In fact, everything about her was dainty. She looked fragile, like a porcelain doll.

A cloud of platinum hair that looked bleached but had been the same color since childhood drifted around that small, perfect face. Big blue eyes, heavily rimmed in black, added to the doll-like appearance. Meg's glitzy silver dress gleamed like sunshine on a mirror when she moved. She began walking purposefully toward them. She even walked like a doll, rather jerkily, due to her extremely high heels.

Robyn put out her arms in welcome. "Meg! Nice to see you again. I was just congratulating Sean on the engagement. I want to wish you well, too."

"Thank you, Robyn." Meg laced her arm possessively through Sean's and smiled up at him. She had to tilt her head way back.

It gave Robyn a moment to check out the engagement ring. She blinked at a brilliant-cut diamond, not quite as big as the Ritz, but huge. She had expected to see the band Sean had given her, and was insensibly relieved not to, even though Meg's ring was obviously more valuable.

"Let's get something to drink, darling. I'm parched," Meg said to Sean. She waved her fingers at Robyn. "We'll get together real soon, Rob. We have so much to talk about." As she spoke she drew Sean away.

He looked back over his shoulder. "See you later, Rob."

Robyn felt a vague sense of frustration, without quite realizing what had caused it. Since when did she and Meg Britten have anything to talk about? They were never friends. The only thing they had in common was Sean Blake, and he would hardly provide an agreeable topic under the circumstances.

Robyn had the satisfaction of noticing how badly matched they were in size. Even in those heels, the tip of Meg's head only came to Sean's shoulder. But that minidoll had an unsuspected will of iron. How neatly she had detached Sean, and he went along like a docile boy. Was that what enraged Robyn? Seeing Sean all tamed and domesticated?

Where had she ever gotten the idea Meg was a rich wimp? When Robyn thought about it, she realized that Meg had always gotten everything she wanted. She wanted to play Mabel in the Gilbert and Sullivan operetta at high school, and she'd done it despite her squeaky voice. Her poor marks should have kept her out of college, but by some means, probably a large donation from her father, she'd been accepted at one of the better schools. And when she decided she wanted Sean Blake, she got him, too.

Now that the first confrontation with Sean was over, Robyn was able to settle down and try to enjoy the party. There were relatives she hadn't seen for years, and she soon got drawn into conversation with them. She caught a glimpse of Sean and Meg from time to time. His height—he was a little taller than most—and Meg's glittery dress made them easy to find, even in the crowded room. But then some heart radar had always enabled Robyn to home in on Sean. She was sure she could find him in the dark.

Later, the young people moved into the next room to dance. It was half a relief that Sean and Meg went along. Jill Halton went, too. It was time for Jill to start executing her plan.

This happened as soon as the music stopped. She went, smiling, up to Meg and Sean. "Will you dance with me, Sean?" she asked with the guile of a child. There were some advantages to being fourteen years old. "Nobody's asked me to dance. I feel like a wall-flower."

"I'd be happy to, Jill. You don't mind, Meg?"

Meg graciously gave permission. She had to go to the ladies' room and fix her face, anyway. The new lipstick, though a superb shade, wore off quickly.

Jill didn't waste any time once she got Sean alone. "Boy, was Robyn ever upset when I told her you were going to be the best man," she said artlessly. "She turned pale as a sheet."

Sean gave a look of disbelief. "She certainly made an amazing recovery!"

"It took a while. Why do you think we were so late? Her eyes didn't still look red, did they? I had a good heart-to-heart talk with her. 'You have to get over him, Robyn,' I said. 'You just have to steel yourself to the fact that you've lost Sean.' Robyn's proud. She didn't want everyone to see how brokenhearted she is."

Sean's brow furrowed, and his jaws moved silently. When he spoke his voice sounded grim. He didn't feel he had to perform in front of a child. "I don't see why *she* should be brokenhearted. She got engaged to Jeff first. Funny she isn't wearing his ring."

Jill bit her lip and considered confessing all but decided to make do with a partial truth. "She isn't exactly engaged yet," she said. Sean would soon know that much, anyway. "Just going steady."

"You told me she was getting the engagement ring for Christmas!" Sean exclaimed.

It was the main reason he'd asked Meg to marry him. Pride demanded retaliation, and Meg happened to be the woman he was going out with at the time. He managed to convince himself he loved her. Every other man in town did. He'd seen a lot of Meg and her family when he took over the Britten Corporation. Meg was beautiful and could make herself very attractive to a man.

Jill scowled. Nothing was working out the way she'd planned. Sean was supposed to be so incensed when she told him that lie about Jeff that he would run straight to Robyn and again ask her to marry him. But what did he do? Propose to stupid old Meg Britten.

"I wouldn't be surprised if she takes the ring when she goes back to Syracuse. Why not, now that you're engaged," she said accusingly.

Sean felt a wild surge of frustration. "Did she say that?" he demanded.

"I couldn't hear everything she said because of the tears. You should be a little kind to her, Sean. Why don't you ask her to dance?"

Sean's eyes narrowed suspiciously. Robyn had never been a crier. He remembered her jaws locked in defiance as she fought back tears when they broke up. But maybe she saved her tears for when she was alone.... His heart wrenched to think of Robyn dissolved in hopeless tears. And there was the added problem of Meg. She was already furious that he had agreed to be Ed Halton's best man. "Are you quite sure this hasn't got something to do with Robyn?" Meg had asked him. Funny how Meg could remind him of a hawk. He hadn't noticed any resemblance before they were engaged. Originally, if he'd had to give a bird simile, he would have said dove. Lately she'd become less gentle.

"She doesn't want to dance with me," Sean said curtly.

"Oh yes, she does!" Jill assured him. "She said 'I hope I can have one last dance with Sean tonight, for old times' sake.' Will Meg not let you?" she asked slyly. At that moment Jill looked remarkably grown up.

"*Let* me?" he asked, rising like a fish to the bait. "She's not my boss."

Jill's air of maturity vanished when she pulled her bottom lip between her teeth and decided she'd set her plan in motion. People would believe almost anything if they wanted to. She was dead certain Sean wanted to believe Robyn still loved him. He wasn't all that eager to believe Meg had him under her dainty white thumb, but Jill would make him see that, too, before long.

"Oh, here's Meg back to claim you," she said when the dance was over. "I guess Rob's out of luck. Too bad."

Jill smiled a sweetly childish smile at Meg and went to look for Robyn.

"I just had a dance with Sean," she announced. "Boy, do I pity that man. Meg's a real shrew. He's dying to ask you to dance."

Robyn's eyes gleamed with interest. "What's stopping him? Meg?" It truly bothered her to see Sean so docile.

"No, I think he'd risk offending her. He's afraid you'd say no. I don't know why he thinks you hate him."

"I don't *hate* him!"

"Really? He seems to think so. I guess he figures you're still mad about that announcement he put in the paper. Why don't you smile at him, or something? Oh, they're serving wine! I'm going to snitch a glass." Jill darted off before Robyn could ask any embarrassing questions.

Robyn stood for a minute, thinking. She didn't want whatever there had been between her and Sean to end in hatred. The end had come suddenly and left a bad taste, but there had been so many good times, too. And in case she decided to come back to Brooktown, it was important to establish normal relations. Sean was a friend of the whole family. She had to be able to meet him without flinching. Really it was childish to go on bickering.

Ed and Noreen strolled up to her. "Do you mind if I borrow the bridegroom for a dance?" Robyn asked. "I promise to bring him back in one piece."

"I guess I can trust him with his own sister." Noreen smiled and handed Ed over.

After their dance Robyn looked around the room for Sean and Meg. She saw Sean looking at her and smiled. He said something to Meg, who pouted. Well, it was too bad if Meg didn't like it. She had some growing up to do, and Robyn was glad to see Sean insisted on his own way.

He came forward, holding Meg by the hand, not quite dragging her. "Your days are numbered, Ed," he joked. "Have you got the last-minute jitters yet?"

"Far from it. I'm looking forward to the big day," Ed assured him. "But while I'm still free, I hope I can induce Meg to dance with me."

Whatever Meg was thinking, she accepted the offer, and when the music began, Sean turned to Robyn. "Dance?" he asked, with a light and easy smile for Meg's benefit.

"You talked me into it."

It felt so strange, being in Sean's arms again. At this close range, she was assailed by a treacherous whiff of the woodsy scent he used. That particular smell would always inundate her with painful memories. It was all so familiar. It almost felt like coming home, except that this particular homecoming of her dreams didn't occur on a crowded dance floor. Instead they'd be alone in some private spot. There was something else wrong, too. Sean was holding her loosely, with a careful inch between them. He never used to dance like that, not with her.

The orchestra was playing the Christmas waltz. They moved gracefully together in time to the music, thighs touching in the swirling motions of the waltz. They'd danced to this very song three years ago at the New Year's ball. She'd worn a long white dress, and afterwards they'd gone home and had mulled wine before the fire. Every detail was etched sharp and deep in her memory, and each memory caused a fresh pain. It was just a week before the big breakup. How happy they'd been that night. That year...

Yes, it would really be too bad to have Sean think she hated him. He'd been a good friend as well as a fiancé. She'd try to remember the friend and forget the hurting lover.

Robyn glanced up at him and smiled softly. Shadows darkened her eyes to glittering hollows and played along the remembered contours of her face. "I really want to be friends with you, Sean."

His arms tightened imperceptibly around her. Now she felt the lean strength of his body against hers. She could even feel his body heat. "What kind of friendship did you have in mind?" he asked with a doubting look.

"Platonic, of course."

"I'm not much good at being a platonic friend with my—with a woman," he finished, and clenched his jaw in annoyance. This was patent nonsense. Robyn knew he had lots of female friends.

"Maybe you can make an exception. Ed wants me to come home and help out with the hotel."

Sean gave a start of surprise. "Come home? But what about Jeff?"

Robyn blinked. "What about him?"

"Will he move his practice to Brooktown?"

"No, of course not."

"Then you're not serious about him?"

"He's a good friend, but we're talking about you."

Sean gave a guarded look. "I think we're talking about *us*, Robyn."

"Yes. It can be uncomfortable when two people who used to—to—" The words stuck in her throat. She hadn't thought it would be so hard to have a normal, rational conversation with Sean.

"To love each other," he said simply. "The word isn't nitroglycerin. You don't have to tiptoe around it."

"Used to be engaged, I was going to say. It's a little uncomfortable being together again after all this time. I was hoping we could establish a—a cordial relationship." Robyn winced at the words that came haltingly from her lips.

Her uncertainty had the strange effect of putting Sean more at his ease. She's more nervous than the bride! he thought. A woman who didn't care about a man didn't act like this. And she'd given old Jeff the heave-ho.

He leaned his head closer and smiled. "You're talking like a bad psychology textbook, Rob. There's no such thing as cordial relations between ex-lovers. If two people can sink to being friends, then whatever it was between them, it wasn't love. When did we ever enjoy cordial relations?" he asked. "In those days we enjoyed laughing and fighting and making up, not very cordially, I might add."

"In those days." It was all ancient history, of course. But it had been that kind of love. Not a quiet, steady warmth, which Ed and Noreen enjoyed, but a blazing fire that blew hot and cold. It was a roller-coaster ride. They squabbled over everything, whether to go to the macho man's movie he wanted to see or the tearjerker romance she favored. Whether Robyn should get her hair cut or keep it long, as Sean liked. He was so stubborn, but she stood up to him. And always in the end there were those wonderful making-up scenes. Until the last time, of course.

It all came washing back over her. Sean's passionate nature made other men seem too tame. He cared so much about everything. And especially, he had cared so much about her. How could he have put that notice in the paper? It was still a mystery after all this time. It didn't fit his usual behavior. Of course he was proud. Maybe his pride had demanded it.

"But now we're all grown up, and we're going to become cordial friends," she said. There, her voice hadn't sounded too breathless, had it?

The laughter dancing in Sean's eyes made a mockery of her poor attempt at civility. "I'm willing to give it a try if you are. With luck we may get through this waltz without a screaming match, but don't push me too far, Robyn. We can't kiss and make up now if it comes to blows," he reminded her.

"I hardly think it'll come to that."

His challenging look pierced her to the core. "You've reformed, have you?"

"I've never hit you!" she exclaimed.

"Ladies have very short memories," Sean murmured, and began humming the Christmas waltz.

Her memory wasn't that short. Robyn remembered very well the one occasion he'd goaded her too far, and she'd slapped his face. It was just one isolated case of complete loss of control. A childish temper tantrum, really.

It had all started when she was late for a date and accepted a ride home with handsome Ned Horton. Sean was at the house waiting for her and saw her get out of Ned's car. Sean was like a wild man, and what really pushed her over the brink was that she was late because she'd been looking for a birthday present for him. Naturally she didn't want to tell him.

She had the engraved lighter right in her purse when he stood, demanding an explanation of why she'd been out with Ned. Sean used to smoke in those days.

He'd quit cold turkey a few months later. He had that kind of willpower. And he'd quit loving her the same way. He was mildly amused by the fact that they were going to be bridesmaid and best man at this wedding, but that's all it was to him. Just an ironic incident.

The dance spun to a stop, and Robyn disengaged herself. "Well, that's all settled then. We are now officially friends. No more fighting."

A smile flashed in the depths of his dark eyes. "And no more kissing and making up. It promises to be a very dull friendship. Thanks for the dance, Rob."

They walked over to Ed and Meg and changed partners.

Chapter Three

The next day was one of those enchanted, fairyland days when new-fallen snow covers the landscape in a pristine blanket of white. Robyn's spirits soared at the sight of snow hung suspended from roof edges, like icing on a cake. It grew on every branch of every tree, twinkling like diamond dust. The glare of sun on white was so strong she wore her sunglasses when she went out shopping for Ed and Noreen's wedding present. Mike had already bought the lamp. A toaster oven was Noreen's second choice. She said she'd be too busy to waste time polishing silver, and she already had her china and crystal. It was a wise choice for a busy working bride.

It was an unromantic gift, but Noreen and Ed were both practical people. Their personalities meshed, and that was the important thing. They'd be happy in the serene way Robyn's parents had been happy in their

love. Robyn couldn't remember ever hearing them
fight. She mused on the mystery of how the right couple came together and got married. That kind of a
calm marriage had its own strength, but it wouldn't
suit her. The thought automatically called up an image of Sean and Meg, and her heart suddenly felt
heavy. The snow that had enchanted her a moment
ago was merely irritating.

She was glad she had so many errands to do. It took
some of the load off her mother and it kept her mind
off a more bothersome subject—Sean. Two hours
later, Robyn checked her list. The toaster oven was in
the trunk of her car, along with the few groceries for
her mom. Ed's suit and Jill's coat from the cleaners
were carefully laid out on the back seat. Robyn decided she'd wear her green alligator pumps with her
bridesmaid gown after all. She couldn't find any silver or gold sandals that fit.

Robyn decided to drop in to the hotel and see if Ed
had a few minutes for a cup of coffee and a visit. It
had been fun shopping in Brooktown where she knew
everyone and could stop in and visit with Ed. That was
the sort of thing she missed in Syracuse—family and
old friends. Of course she had made new friends in
Syracuse, but it wasn't the same. They didn't have a
whole lifetime of memories to share. It was like entering a second home when she pushed open the grilled
glass door of the Halton Hotel.

Ed took advantage of the visit to try to lure Robyn
back to Brooktown. "Why don't you come up and
have a look at the suite you'd be using if you decided
to come back?" he said temptingly. "I know you
wouldn't want to go home to live again. It's hard to be

an adult when you live at home with Mom. She does tend to keep an eye on the clock when you're out at night. This way you'd be close, without being back under the maternal thumb.''

"That sounds like the voice of experience. Lead on," Robyn said.

They took the elevator up to the top floor. In this new addition, the smell of lumber and paint still hung in the air. The carpet and walls were unmarked by wear. The Halton Hotel was only four stories high, but the window at the end of the hall gave a sweeping view of the bustling city below. Cars and pedestrians stood out in lively array against the new-fallen snow. At the bottom of Main Street, the river flowed gently by in summer. Even in winter it was alive. Kids were taking advantage of the Christmas holiday to have a game of hockey. Brooktown would be a good place to settle down and raise a family.

"This floor's nice and quiet," Ed said. "Sean put the larger and more expensive suites up here. You wouldn't hear much noise from the clients. It's mostly businessmen."

He unlocked one of the end doors and showed Robyn in. "This is the living room. It looks bare," he said, before she could voice the thought herself. "I left the decorating till you decide. You could paper the white walls. I chose the blue carpet with you in mind. I know your penchant for blue."

Robyn's love of blue was so well known that her family and close friends teased her about it. It was one of the things she and Sean hadn't argued about. He liked blue, too, even if it didn't match her eyes.

"The bedroom's in here," Ed said, and crossed the room to a closed door. When he opened it, Robyn saw the bedroom had been furnished with a matching teak dresser, desk and bed. She mentally added her own accessories. It would make a charming apartment.

"The bathroom isn't quite finished," Ed mentioned. "Sean's putting a double-mirrored vanity over the sink. You can have a look—"

They were interrupted by the phone. Ed answered it and said, "Okay, I'll be right down." He turned to Robyn. "I've got to go now. A biggish ski party's just arrived. I want to welcome them personally. Take your time, Rob. Look around. If you want to change anything, Sean's still working on it, so it isn't impossible to make a few changes."

Ed noticed that Sean's name made his sister uncomfortable. "You aren't still bothered by the Sean thing, are you?" he asked.

Robyn made the necessary face-saving lie. "No, of course not."

"I didn't think so. That was years ago. I really don't think you have to worry that he'd bother you, Rob. He's gotten over it. And now that he's getting married—well, Meg will keep him on a pretty tight leash."

"You'd better get down to the guests," Robyn said.

She was glad to be left alone. Ed's interpretation of her concern over Sean intrigued her. He thought Sean might still care, after what he'd done. How could a brother be so blind? Didn't it show that she still cared about him more than she should? What she often felt was miles removed from love, but it certainly wasn't indifference. That was the real test, when you could stop caring at all about someone. Would her feelings die a natural death after he married Meg?

At least Sean had stopped caring about her. His feelings needn't stand in the way of her coming home. This visit confirmed her decision that it was time to do just that. Everyone and everything she cared about were here, where she'd been born and had grown up. It was good for young adults to have a taste of freedom, to leave home and meet new people and try new experiences, to complete the last painful step of growing up. But when the growing was finished, you should be able to come home. Damn Sean Blake, anyway!

She wouldn't let him stop her. Ed needed her here. Once the hotel was completely finished, Sean's friendship with her family would probably peter out. She wouldn't have to see much of him and Meg.

Robyn walked to the window. This one looked down on city hall. Its copper dome, which had weathered to a dull verdigris, showed through where the snow was already melting in the sun. Sean's restorations weren't visible from this angle, but she'd seen them already. The old stone building that gave the town character looked as it had a hundred years ago when it was built. The clock in the tower once more tolled the hour for the convenience of shoppers.

The benches under the trees in front of the hall were empty today. Nobody wanted to sit in the snow, so they stood on the corner, stamping their feet as they waited for the bus. She saw Judge Corcoran hurrying into the building. Ed and Noreen used to talk about getting married at city hall. She was glad they'd opted for a more traditional wedding. Meg would want a

great, elaborate do. Would Robyn be invited if she
came home? Invited to see Sean swear eternal love to
another woman?

Robyn heard a key in the lock and turned around,
surprised that Ed had come back so soon. Her surprise surged to tumult when Sean Blake stepped into
the room. It felt as if her thoughts had conjured him
up. Dismay lent a rough edge to her voice.

"What are you doing here?" she demanded.
"Where'd you get that key?"

Sean gave a startled look. "I'm still working on this
suite. I dropped Meg off for a coffee downstairs and
decided to double-check the measurements for the
vanity while I'm here."

Robyn knew her reaction had been too strong. It
revealed that she was acutely interested in Sean, and
his questioning look told her he had noticed it. Her
temper wasn't assuaged to hear he'd been with Meg,
but she tried to soften her first exclamation.

"Oh, of course. Ed mentioned it. Sorry I snapped
at you."

"I won't bother you. I'll be out of here in a minute."

Sean strode briskly to the bathroom, pulling a
measuring tape from his pocket as he went. His cheeks
were ruddy from the cold, and his black hair was
windblown. Sean's rugged style looked almost better
in work clothes than in a suit. His fleece-lined leather
jacket emphasized the width of his shoulders. Even in
jeans and work boots, he looked terrific. He used to
be sensitive about calling on her in his work clothes.

"Your folks probably think you're going out with a blue-collar bum," he'd said once. "Your dad always looks dressed for a visit to the White House."

"We're not that snobbish! And blue-collar workers aren't bums, for heaven's sake."

"I'm not a blue-collar worker," he'd added swiftly. "I *own* Blake Construction Company. I'm a capitalist like your Dad, even if I do get my hands dirty sometimes."

They'd fought about that, too. She tried to convince Sean that *he* was the snob. It didn't matter to her what he wore or what he did for a job, as long as it was honest work. She knew he was still sensitive about his interrupted education. That crack last night about Jeff being an Ivy League lawyer proved it.

In less than a minute, Sean came out. "All finished," he said, sliding the tape into his pocket.

Robyn was determined to set her relationship with Sean on an even keel and decided to take advantage of this opportunity.

"You did a good job on the expansion, Sean. It's lovely."

"Thanks. I thought you might come and have a look while the work was in progress," he replied. His words said indirectly that he'd at least noticed her absence. His tone hinted that he'd like to hear the reason.

"I was pretty busy," she said vaguely.

He glanced around the room. "The ceiling moldings were my idea. They add a touch of class, I think, and the cost is minimal. Nowadays you can buy them prefabricated in the old traditional designs."

Robyn looked at them, nodding. "I always think wallpaper looks a bit funny without moldings. Of course you can use a border, but the molding will look nicer when I get it papered."

Sean gave her a curious, questioning look. "Are you going to decorate the room for Ed?" he asked.

"No, for me."

Sean's brow puckered in a frown, and his eyes flashed dangerously. This was the look she'd expected last night when they first met. What had she said to earn it now? She'd often seen that look in the past. It usually meant a fight was brewing between them. It used to frighten her a little, but she was older now and more sure of herself. And she didn't have to worry about his feelings. She no longer had anything to lose.

She watched as Sean's jaw tightened and his face assumed a veneer of indifference. When he spoke his voice was stiff. "What's that supposed to mean?"

Robyn's heart thudded heavily as the blood throbbed through her veins. "I told you Ed wants me to come back and help him run the hotel. I'll be staying here. I'm used to my privacy now. I'm not sure I want Mom to be clocking me in and out of the house."

A blaze of blue fire leaped from his eyes. "You're not coming back here!"

Robyn's heartbeats quickened to the challenge. "Who's going to stop me? I can see by your placards that you're rebuilding the town. I didn't hear you own it."

"I don't want you here!" He clenched his fists.

"Then you'll have to buy a rail and run me out of town. I've decided to stay." A thrill of nervous triumph quivered through her. So she could still get Sean into a rage! What happened to his indifference?

"Why?" His question was a howl of protest. "Why here? Go to New York. Go to Chicago. But don't come back here."

It seemed to Robyn almost unfair to use the tricks learned from loving Sean to anger him now. She knew just what to say, just how to act to infuriate him, and infuriating him was exactly what she wanted to do. How dare he give her an ultimatum? "What's the matter, Sean? Isn't this town big enough for both of us? Or are you afraid Meg will object?" she asked with a mocking smile.

"This has nothing to do with Meg!"

"You're right. This has nothing to do with Meg or with you. It's my decision. I've decided to come back," she stated firmly. She lifted her head high and stared as Sean's flaring nostrils quivered a moment. Then he grinned cynically.

"You always knew how to push my buttons, didn't you, Robyn?"

"Robots run on buttons. I was hoping you'd changed."

"I *have* changed. You won't find me as easy to lead by the nose as you used to."

"Unlike bulls, men should be amenable to reason. But actually I have no desire or intention of leading you anywhere, except, hopefully, out that door." She pointed an imperative finger to the door. "Easy to lead!" Was the man insane? When had it ever been easy to deal with Sean Blake?

Sean looked at her pointing finger. He looked at the door and then crossed his arms and planted his feet a foot apart to show he meant to stay. The pose infuriated her.

"We might as well get this out in the open once and for all," Sean said.

"I'm not hiding any dark secrets."

"You didn't tell me why you're coming back."

"There's a reason why I didn't. It's none of your business, but since you imagine there's some scheme afoot, I'll tell you. Ed needs help running the hotel now that it's expanded. It's partly mine. I always intended to work here. I've decided this is the time to return. Does that answer your question?"

A glint of amusement gleamed in his eyes, and a knowing smile parted his lips. "You're doing it again, aren't you? You thought Jeff was going to pop the question at Christmas. He didn't, so you're running away, leaving town, trying to scare him into marrying you."

Robyn was literally speechless at this wild misinterpretation. She stared, trying to make sense of it. The first item to fall into place was that telltale "doing it again." He meant she'd left Brooktown in the first place in an effort to scare *him* into line. That's what the conceited oaf really believed. Didn't he realize the shame she felt when her fiancé publicly repudiated her?

"I could have Jeff Perkins by snapping my fingers," she boasted. "I never run away from a challenge."

"Don't you?" he taunted. "Then *you've* changed. You ran away when I didn't buckle under about taking that job with Britten and buying a house I couldn't afford."

"You're forgetting a few details. I left town because everybody and his dog was laughing at me after you put that announcement in the paper." Robyn's voice rose as she mentally relived that hellish period. And here was the cause of it all, standing in front of her, sneering!

Sean's voice was equally loud when he said, "Somebody had to do it. You didn't."

"It was hardly the man's job!"

"You gave back the ring, and you wouldn't take my calls or answer the door. When something's over, it's over. I like to wrap up all the details. It didn't seem to occur to you a lot of people still thought we were engaged."

"You were having a spot of trouble getting dates, was that it?" she flashed back.

"It was my way of telling you I wasn't going to back down and buy that house I couldn't afford."

"You could have afforded it if you'd taken the job!"

"Yes, if I'd sold my soul," he growled. "I didn't want to build five hundred split-levels, all alike except for the door or the color of brick. Take a look around this town, now that you insist on coming back. See what I've done to Brooktown. You'll see beautiful, authentic restorations. And the new church—the architects couldn't find any other builder who could or would do that kind of stonework. I don't slap up tomorrow's slums. I build *quality*. Nothing was going to change that. Not even *you*."

It was the closest Sean had ever come to boasting, and the first time he'd ever really explained why he wouldn't take the job with Britten. Why hadn't he told her before? Did he think she couldn't understand anything except money?

Robyn knew he was already sorry he'd revealed so much. His fury had subsided to frustration. "Anyway, that has nothing to do with it," he said, dismissing the subject.

But it had a lot to do with it. For the first time, Robyn understood his obstinacy over the job and the little brick cottage on the river. She felt a swell of regret that was mirrored in her eyes. His speech threw new light on that newspaper announcement, too. Sean had considered it final; it had been his frustrated effort to make her face facts.

"You never told me that before," she said.

His voice was rough, but not with anger. It was some gentler emotion that echoed there. "Did I overestimate your intelligence? I seem to remember telling you I didn't want to spend the rest of my life building split-levels."

Yes, he'd said that, but not with the passion of today's outburst and not with the fuller explanation of what he *did* want to build. A moment of self-conscious knowledge hovered in the air between them.

"So why did you buy out Britten?" she asked.

"I bought his equipment and hired his men when he wanted to retire. That's all. We seem to have strayed from the original point. You're coming back to help Ed out with the hotel, then. It's definite?"

"Yes," she said, but she was already besieged by doubts.

Robyn wanted to think about what she'd learned today. The excitement of the argument was over, but it left her only confused and uncertain. That wasn't how their arguments usually ended, at an impasse with no kissing and making up. Maybe coming back wasn't such a good idea, because she really wanted very much to kiss Sean.

The atmosphere was tense, and it felt as if they stood in an invisible magnetic field that drew them inexorably together. If they had to stay apart, then being around Brooktown was a very bad idea. Three years of absence hadn't cured her. She knew Sean's presence would do the job.

She glanced at him, wondering why he didn't look at her. Sean seemed even more uncertain than she felt herself. He looked out the window. "It's really none of my business where you decide to live, or why. But I think it would be—better if you didn't come back right now," he said stiffly.

"Why?" It was the logical question. Why did he care so much where she lived?

Sean turned away from the window slowly and met her gaze. She saw the troubled shadow in his eyes. The anger was gone now. Sean's rages never lasted long. It looked like a shadow of regret. His voice sounded wistful. "Why do you think?"

He didn't wait for an answer. He just turned on his heel and strode quickly out of the room. His departure had the air of an escape from danger. Robyn stood alone, wondering. She was beginning to think she wasn't the only one who still cared. It appeared that Sean wasn't quite over her, either. He was afraid of what would happen if they were together much.

This added another obstacle to her return. Yet every instinct urged her to come home. It was impossible for her to leave before the wedding in any case, so she had a few more days before making her final decision.

When Ed didn't come back to the suite, Robyn went down to the lobby to say goodbye. Jill was there with her arms full of parcels. She bared a timmy smile.

"Great post-Christmas sales!" she beamed. "I got two sweaters for the price of one with the money Aunt Lee gave me for Christmas."

"Good. You can show me when we get home. Do you want a lift?" Robyn asked. "I've got the car outside."

"I'm going to have a sandwich at the coffee shop," Jill replied. "Mom's out getting her hair done. She's not cooking lunch today, and I don't want to make myself another turkey sandwich."

Robyn felt the same way, so they went to the coffee shop together.

"There's Meg Britten," Jill mentioned, and nodded toward a booth.

Robyn knew Sean had left Meg here but thought she would have gone by now. Meg spotted them and stood up to wave. "Robyn—over here. Come and join me. I'm all alone."

Meg was about the last person Robyn wanted to talk to, but it was impossible to ignore her summons. Meg always liked to be noticed and had shouted loud enough that half the customers turned to look at her. She looked stunning, as usual. Her fragile appearance was emphasized by a black turtleneck sweater that fit like a tent. Slender black leather pants and high boots completed the outfit.

"I'm glad I ran into you," Meg said brightly. "I forgot to sell you tickets to *Pygmalion*. The Brooktown Dramatic Society's putting it on next week."

Robyn felt a snide urge to say, I know. Sean told me. That would open up Meg's eyes. But of course she didn't say it. "I'd love to see it, but I won't be here next week. I'm going back to Syracuse on Monday."

"Oh, but you can buy a couple of tickets, anyway, to support the dramatic society. I'm playing Liza Doolittle." Meg smiled. "Did anyone tell you I'm the president of the society now?" As she spoke she pulled a pair of tickets form her purse and handed them to Robyn—with her left hand. The big diamond twinkled.

"No, I hadn't heard."

"My picture was in the paper when I was elected," Meg said, her lips set in a pout of disappointment at Robyn's ignorance.

"Would you like to go, Jill?" Robyn asked.

"Sure! I bet Mom would, too. She loved *My Fair Lady*."

Robyn bought two tickets and gave them to her sister.

They ordered a sandwich, and while they ate, Meg rattled on about the play. "George Bernard Shaw writes such marvelous lines. I was disappointed to see he left out so many of the great scenes from the movie."

Jill gave a light cough and smiled at Robyn.

"You know what I mean!" Meg laughed. "I know Shaw wrote the play first. I wish we'd chosen the musical *My Fair Lady* instead. I'm taking singing lessons, so we might tackle that another year. I thought

I'd never master the cockney accent, but as luck would have it, our maid speaks cockney English. She was actually born within the sound of the bells of St. Mary-le-Bow, so my accent is authentic.''

"Loverly," Jill said, smiling into her sandwich.

"For the first part, I'm wearing an old, raggedy, dusty coat and putting actual mud in my hair." Meg laughed. "It's going to be a panic backstage. Between acts I have to have the hairdresser wash my hair and set it. And the costumes! You *must* see my gowns, Robyn.''

"I'm sorry I won't be able to go to the play," Robyn repeated.

"You can still see the clothes. I have them all at the house. Sean's new house, I mean," she added brightly. "He's letting us use it for rehearsals and to store props. We really must get up a committee to raise funds for a permanent home for the dramatic society.''

"Sean bought a house!" Robyn exclaimed. She hadn't heard about that. She was curious to see it but didn't want to risk running into him again.

"Yes, that old brick house by the river, part of the Rinehart estate. It's not actually ready to live in yet. We're making some improvements before we move in. You know Sean. A few of us are having a rehearsal there this afternoon. Our big rehearsals with all the cast are held at night. Why don't you drop around now?''

Her house! Sean had bought the brick cottage on the river for Meg. Robyn felt desolate, as if Meg had stolen her child. "I'm afraid I don't have time," she said coolly.

"It would only take a minute. It's right on our way home," Jill urged.

"Perfect. You can drop me off," Meg said. It seemed churlish to refuse. "I got a lift downtown with Sean. My Mercedes is in the garage. Honestly, you pay a fortune for a car, and then somebody goes and rear ends you." She gave a tsk of annoyance.

"I can certainly drop you off at least," Robyn agreed.

She was consumed with curiosity to see what improvements Sean was making to her house. "That old brick house by the river, part of the Rinehart estate." It had to be the house she'd wanted him to buy. Had he no feelings for her at all, that he could live there with another woman, in their house? She felt betrayed. She thought he'd kept the original engagement ring for sentimental reasons, but he hadn't. Meg probably just wanted a showier ring.

They all went to the car, and when they got to the wrought-iron gates that led into the Rinehart estate, Robyn stopped.

"You can drive right up to the house," Meg said.

"Which one is it?" she asked, and sat, clenching the wheel with white knuckles. She shouldn't go. She shouldn't even ask, but an overwhelming curiosity was rapidly swelling to compulsion.

If Meg said the little cottage that used to be the Rinehart guest house, Robyn didn't think she could hold in her tears. Below, a new street had been put in perpendicular to the river, with about a dozen modern houses. They weren't on the water but within view of it.

"I told you, it's the Rinehart house," Meg said rather impatiently.

"You mean the *mansion*?"

Meg smiled contentedly. "You didn't think I'd live in one of those ticky-tacky bungalows, did you? Even if my dad did build them. They're cute, but Sean and I wanted something grander. Call us pretentious!" She laughed. "Come on in. I'm a little early. I don't see any other cars here yet, so I'll show you around."

Robyn felt light with relief. Not *her* house, not *her* engagement ring on Meg's finger. Gaudier and more expensive substitutes in both cases, but at least not hers. A quick look showed Robyn that Sean's Porsche wasn't there. She wasn't likely to have another chance to see the house, and with Jill urging her, she agreed.

She felt a sting of jealousy when Meg pulled out the key. The house was quite simply magnificent. It had once stood in four acres of private park. Three of the acres had been severed for the bungalows, but the house still had a large private lot. Although it had been built as a summer home for the millionaire Rineharts, it was no cottage. It stood three stories high, with a small dome on top. The pretty little round windows must be in the attic, Robyn figured.

She felt as if she were entering a hotel when Meg unlocked the door and she stepped into a vast hallway tiled in Connemara marble. Meg gave another tsk of annoyance. "Sean must have been here. I notice the heat's been turned down," she said, and went to adjust the thermostat. "He's using the master bedroom as an office while he's working on the renovations."

Meg's temporary departure gave Robyn a minute to look around. The first thing she noticed was the beautiful curved staircase. The post at the bottom was in the form of a lion's head, but it was at the newly laid carpet that she stared questioningly. It was done in a dusty blue, a color that Robyn always considered peculiarly her own. Sean knew she loved that color. Of course he liked it too, and it would certainly flatter Meg's coloring. While she stood thinking, Jill darted off to the right, and Robyn followed her.

There was some scaffolding in the study there. A quick peek showed Robyn the ceiling was being painted. The walls of paneled oak were beautiful. Bookcases were built in along one wall and a fieldstone fireplace was at the end. Robyn imagined herself curled up in front of that fireplace on a cold winter's night, with a cup of hot cocoa. The wind from the river would blow in vain against the sturdy walls, with her and Sean safe and warm inside. Except that it wouldn't be her with Sean. It would be Meg.

"In here," Meg called from across the hallway, and Robyn went to join her.

"Can I go upstairs?" Jill asked.

"Don't you want to see the costumes?" Meg said.

"Later," Jill replied, and scampered upstairs to examine the bedrooms.

Meg uncovered a clothes rack and held up an ornate silk gown. "This is what I wear in the final scene," she said. "When Liza sweeps out the door, saying, 'What you are to do without me I cannot imagine.' Liza doesn't marry her Professor Higgins, you know. You'd be surprised how many people think she does. Shaw has a marvelous piece at the end of the play. It isn't spoken, but I think it should be. It explains how Higgins will always think of her as a flower girl and treat her badly. Liza marries Freddie Eynsford Hill—Joe Scanlon's playing the part—because he just plain adores her.''

"She probably does the right thing."

"She does the practical thing, but it isn't very romantic. However, we can't very well take liberties with GBS. The spoken ending is quite ambiguous, actually. Everyone will think Liza and Henry are going to get together. The play ends with Henry Higgins laughing his head off.''

Meg hung the gown up again and selected another. "And this is what I wear in act 3.''

While ostensibly admiring the gowns, Robyn cast quick looks around the room. This was the formal living room. The molded plaster lent it an air of elegance. The only furnishings were a few old upholstered pieces that came with the house. When Meg had shown her all her outfits, she too looked at the room.

"The house is really ridiculously large," she said, "but it will be great for parties. I'm sure I could get a hundred guests in here. The cast parties have a way of growing.''

"At least a hundred."

"I'm going to do the walls in a heavy embossed white-and-gold paper. I'm having a prewedding party here.''

Robyn's insides shrank to think of that wedding. Less and less did it seem possible for her to come back to Brooktown. "When do you plan to get married?'' she asked, trying for a casual air.

"As soon as Sean can get the house fixed up. Probably in the spring. I'd like a June wedding. I want to wear a long white-satin gown, with an old-fashioned headpiece that comes down in a peak over my forehead. I saw one in a bridal shop in New York. It looked fantastic on me."

Meg's face wore the dreamy look of a woman in love when she talked about the wedding. It was the same expression she'd worn when she was displaying her gowns for the play. Robyn noticed that all her plans were voiced in the first person. "I" am going to do this and that, not "we." Meg might have a surprise in store if she thought Sean would let her have it all her own way.

"I'm having six bridesmaids," she continued. "Do you think different pastel shades would be nice, or the six of them all in the same color?"

"Either way. Why don't you ask the bridesmaids what they'd like?"

"It's my wedding!" Meg pointed out with that little pout that came so easily to her face. "On that one day at least I should have things the way I want. It'll be the most important day of my life. Everyone will be looking at me."

"Sean wants a big wedding, does he?"

"Of course. He thinks ritual is important. And besides, Dad's paying for everything, so he can't object."

This sounded to Robyn as if Sean might have been less than enthusiastic. Meg talked a little more about the wedding. She discussed the flowers, and her going-away outfit and the reception. As Robyn listened she noticed that while the wedding loomed large, the word "marriage" wasn't used once. It was the spectacle of it that interested Meg. Another leading role for her to play. She didn't want a marriage, she wanted a wedding.

When they heard a car drive up outside, Robyn hurried to the window, certain that Sean was going to catch her. It was a blue Volvo carrying four people. She was happy to get away. "Your fellow actors are arriving. I'll run along now. Where's Jill got to?"

Jill came running down the stairs. "What a great house!" she exclaimed. "It has eight bedrooms, Rob, and a marble bathroom with a big tub standing on lion's feet. Neat."

"The bathrooms are the first thing to be renovated!" Meg said firmly. "I want a platform tub with a Jacuzzi."

"You can't take out that tub!" Jill objected. "A platform whirlpool would look stupid in that old-fashioned room."

"It won't be old-fashioned when I get through with it," Meg said. "And this blue carpet on the stairs will have to go, too."

"Why?" Jill asked with a little smile at her sister.

"You'd never know it was new. It looks dusty. Poor Sean had it installed before we got engaged. Thank heavens he didn't do any other decorating."

"Robyn always liked this shade of blue," Jill said with an innocent look. Robyn glared her to silence.

The door burst open at that moment, and a group of actors came in. "Darlings!" Meg smiled and went to greet them. "You're all late. And you, Professor Higgins, let's hear your accent." She smiled over her shoulder. "Bye girls. Thanks for the lift. We'll see you tomorrow night at the wedding rehearsal."

Robyn recognized some of the other actors. They recognized her, too, and looked surprised to find her with Meg. That should give them all something interesting to gossip about! The sisters let themselves out.

"I didn't know Sean had bought that house," Jill said. "He must be rich. Or maybe Meg's Dad is paying for part of it."

"Sean wouldn't let him. He likes to be the boss." He wouldn't even let her father give them a down payment.

"He won't boss Meg Britten. I bet she'll rip out that neat tub and put in a pink Jacuzzi. You should have seen it, Rob. It had brass faucets. There were funny brass rails along the wall, too. I wonder what they're for."

"They're probably towel warmers. Some of the old houses have them."

"I'd like to have a house like that when I grow up and get married."

"Who wouldn't?" Robyn said forlornly.

"It's funny we didn't hear he'd bought it. The date of purchase said October 15."

"Jill, were you snooping in Sean's private papers?"

"Not snooping, exactly. They were right on the desk in the master bedroom. He paid—"

"I don't want to hear it. It's wrong to read other people's private correspondence." Robyn stifled her curiosity. She did ask one question, however. "When did Sean start going out with Meg?"

"At the end of October. I remember Meg was going out with Dr. Lattimer when school started back. Ed thought she'd marry him, but he got back with his wife instead. His wife teaches me English. It wasn't until Halloween that Mrs. Lattimer stopped yelling at us in class. We wondered why she didn't give Buck Reilly a detention for putting on that gorilla mask in class. Then we found out she was in a good mood because she'd just got back together with her husband. Why did you want to know, Rob?'' she asked slyly.

"Just curious.'' If Sean bought the house before he started seeing Meg, then he hadn't bought it for her. "They didn't go together long before they got engaged, did they?''

"Meg's a fast worker.''

"Of course they've known each other for years.''

But at least it wasn't Meg's work that made Sean buy the Rinehart house. Robyn was insensibly pleased that he'd done it by himself. She didn't want to think of him being led around by Meg. And Meg didn't have anything to do with that blue carpet on the front stairs, either. Is it even remotely conceivable that Sean bought that particular house with *me* in mind? Robyn thought.

When they were in the car, Jill sat biting her bottom lip. She carefully crossed her fingers inside her pockets and said in a confidential voice, "You know what, Rob? Sean has a picture of you in his bedroom. It's not in a frame or anything, but there's a little picture of you in the top drawer of the desk. I hope Meg doesn't see it. There's no picture of her there.''

Robyn felt the blood rush from her face, leaving her light-headed. Her heart felt swollen with love and sorrow.

Jill risked a quick glance at her sister. "I think he still loves you,'' she added daringly. "It's too bad he proposed to Meg. I bet he wouldn't have if he'd known you were coming back to Brooktown.''

"I'm not coming back, Jill."

"Why not!" Jill exclaimed, her topaz eyes wide in shock.

"I just don't think it's a good idea."

Jill bit back a smile and said in a confidential voice, "You still love him, don't you, Rob?"

"Don't be ridiculous! And don't you *dare* tell anyone he has my picture in his room."

"I won't."

Robyn tried to withhold the next question, but she was only human, and she had to know. "What picture was it?"

"The one of you and him together on the sofa at home. The one Ed took the day you got engaged. I wonder what he did with the ring. It isn't the one Meg's wearing. He gave you his mother's engagement ring, remember?" A quick peep showed her Rob remembered very well. "I guess Meg probably wanted a bigger diamond, huh?"

Robyn didn't answer. Her throat was clogged with tears.

Chapter Four

Jill Halton flopped down on her bed, put her earphones to her ears and closed her eyes to help her to think. She'd learned a few useful items from the lunch with Meg. If she attended long rehearsals for *Pygmalion* most evenings, when did she see Sean? They couldn't see too much of each other, and that was a shame. Jill was sure familiarity would breed contempt.

A way to open Sean's eyes was to throw him together with Robyn. It would have to be done in an underhanded manner. She'd often seen Sean skating at the rink the town cleared off on the river. He refereed hockey games there, and when the game was over at eight, he sometimes stayed to skate. He probably would stay if Robyn was there, and Robyn liked skating.

Jill rose from the bed, pulled on one of the new sweaters and went to Robyn's room. Her sister was examining a white flower attached to a piece of veil.

"Oh, hi, Jill. That's one of the new sweaters, huh?" Jill uncovered her ears and Robyn said, "The Sandbaggers?"

"Nope. They don't go with my new sweaters. Too earthy."

"It's a nice color. Red really suits you. Unfortunately this headpiece for the wedding doesn't suit me. The band's so tight it could crack my skull. I wonder how I can stretch it."

"Use the pliers. That's what I did with mine."

"A good idea."

"What are you doing tonight, Rob?"

"Not much. Do you want to go to a movie?"

"There's nothing good on. I really need some exercise after my Christmas pig out."

"I don't want to jog at night and in winter."

"Jog?" Jill asked, shocked. "If God wanted us to go more than three miles an hour, he'd have given us wheels. Would you like to go skating? I bet you don't get to go skating in Syracuse."

"Sure, I often do. They have a rink there. I'd like to go with you, but I didn't bring my skates home."

"You could wear Noreen's. She left them here after she went skating with me and Ed last Sunday afternoon. She wouldn't mind."

"I don't suppose she would. All right, I'll go with you. It will be fun."

"Great. Public skating starts at eight, after the hockey game." Jill left without saying a word about who refereed the game.

Robyn adjusted her headband with the pliers. Then she went to help her mother make dinner. It was becoming clearer by the minute that she couldn't come back to Brooktown to live, so she wanted to spend as much time as possible with her family. She enjoyed their company, and it helped keep at bay her regrets about Sean. She made a strong effort to behave as though nothing was bothering her. With the wedding to distract them, neither Ed nor Mrs. Halton noticed anything amiss. She fooled everyone but Jill.

Jill knew the timing of their arrival at the rink was crucial. If they went before the hockey game was over, Rob would see Sean and might go home. On the other hand, they couldn't get there too long after the game, or Sean might have left. The city was really strict about public skating starting at eight sharp, so Jill decided they should arrive at eight. She'd make sure Sean knew they were there, if she had to go into the clubhouse and confront him.

By merciless badgering of her sister, Jill got Robyn out the door of home at ten to eight. She was glad to see Robyn had taken some pains with her dressing. Sean would remember that bulky white sweater and the red quilted vest Rob wore over it. The knitted band she wore to protect her ears was attractive. It threw Rob's high cheekbones into prominence.

Jill looked the outfit over with satisfaction, except for one detail. "Your hands will be cold in gloves. Don't you have any mittens?"

"Not with me. I can warm up in the clubhouse. Let's go."

The players were just leaving the ice when they got there. "You go on in and put on your skates," Jill suggested. "I want to show Norma McIntyre my new sweater." Jill wore the red sweater under her jacket.

Sean was talking to the goalie when Jill went to the rink. "Hi, Sean." She smiled brightly. "Are you staying to skate?"

"I'll have a few rounds. It's a nice night—not too cold."

"Will you skate with me?" she asked, and smiled saucily. "I want to make my girlfriends jealous."

Sean shook his head. "Beware, my dear. Flattery will get you anywhere. You women are all alike. I'll be around for a while, if you hurry."

When Jill entered the clubhouse, Robyn looked up from lacing her skates. "Hurry up, slowpoke!"

"Don't wait for me, Rob. I'll be out in a minute."

Robyn stood up. "See you at the rink," she said, and went out the door, eager for a skate.

The path to the rink was rough. The river was a few yards below ground level, and the slope was usually negotiated by sliding on your bottom. As most of the skaters were teenagers, this presented no problem, but Robyn was a little embarrassed.

She was just picking herself up when a leather-gloved hand reached out to help her. "Thank you," she said, and when she glanced up, she found herself looking into Sean Blake's amused face, and her smile froze. He pulled her rather roughly to her feet. Her skate slipped and she bumped against his chest. Sean automatically reached out to steady her.

"Sean!" That first surprised exclamation sounded too joyful, and she consciously changed her tone. "What are you doing here?" she demanded. The wild idea darted into her head that he'd come looking for her.

He held her firmly by the wrists while she gained her balance. It brought their heads close together. "I have to be someplace. This morning you were shocked to find me doing my job at the hotel. Now you're hinting that the public rink is out-of-bounds. Where's a guy supposed to go?" A glint of mockery entered his eyes. "I'll give you fair warning, so that we can avoid these unwanted meetings. Tomorrow I'll be in my office. I'd appreciate it if you didn't demand what I'm doing there, if you happen to run into me."

"That's not very likely, is it?" she said, and pulled away, noticing that Sean didn't let go. His fingers clung to her hands as she withdrew them.

Sean gave her a sardonic look. "You mean you're not following me?"

"Be real." She laughed and felt as childish as she knew she sounded.

Two or three teenagers were waiting impatiently to descend the slide to the rink. "Why don't you two talk someplace else!" one loud-voiced boy shouted, and they moved aside.

"Sean, if I'd had a single suspicion you'd be here—" No, Robyn thought. She wouldn't give him the satisfaction of thinking he had anything to do with her actions.

His knowing smile told her he'd mentally finished the sentence. Sean always understood her uncomfortably well. "Is that the way platonic friends behave in Syracuse?" he asked, unfazed. In fact he was enjoying her chagrin.

"Some friends are best enjoyed in absentia."

"That can only mean you enjoy your memories of them. Obviously I'm not that kind of friend."

"You've got that right."

"Because you're not satisfied with just a memory of me. You must have had at least one little suspicion that I might be at my own house today when you went there?" he taunted.

Robyn gave a mental wince at that piece of folly. And of course Meg had to tell him! "Meg asked me to give her a lift."

"You could have refused."

"Why should I?" she asked. "It was on my way home."

"And you were curious to see my house. Admit it now, just between us—friends."

"I was curious," she agreed, and watched as his smile spread in satisfaction. "I was always curious to get a look at the Rinehart mansion," she added blandly, and had the exquisite satisfaction of watching his smile fade.

"We call it the Blake mansion now," he retaliated.

"Very grand, Sean. You'll have to give up your role as poor little blue-collar boy, now that you've bought the most expensive house in Brooktown."

"It wasn't that expensive. It needs work. I happen to know a guy that's in that line," he added facetiously. He looked over her shoulder and waved. "Excuse me. My date's here. See you around—if we're not both careful." Then he skated away.

Robyn's temper was ragged, and it got even worse when she thought Meg was here. She looked after Sean and was surprised to see Jill taking his arm. Jill, his "date?" Had Jill arranged this meeting? A cloud

gathered on Robyn's brow. Her instinct was to jump
into her car and drive home, but she wouldn't satisfy
Sean by doing it. She'd come to skate, and she'd skate.
Sean Blake would not change her normal behavior by
one iota.

The wind on the river was cold, but Robyn's emotions kept her warm. She was careful to stay behind
Jill and Sean. It surprised her to see them getting along
so well. They kept up a bantering conversation while
they sailed along the ice. What on earth did they find
to talk about? The only thing they had in common was
her. Then she remembered the hotel expansion and
Ed's wedding, and felt chastened. Naturally that was
what they were talking about. Why did she imagine
Sean was always thinking of her?

Robyn knew she was handling the Sean issue very
badly. She shouldn't jump like a startled rabbit every
time she saw him, and ask what he was doing there. It
was the painful lurching of her heart that caused it.
She couldn't show her joy, so she had to simulate anger.

She shouldn't have gone into his house with Meg. If
he thought she went in hope of seeing him, he was
wrong. It had only been vulgar curiosity. She wanted
to see where he and Meg would be living. Why should
she even be curious about it? Sean was nothing to her
now. At least he should be nothing.

But if he were nothing, she wouldn't be carrying this
heavy heart around inside her chest. She wouldn't be
wishing it was *her* arm he was holding on to while he
talked and laughed so merrily. Why wasn't he with
Meg? And since he wasn't with Meg, why was he with
Jill? *Was* it because Jill was her sister?

Robyn thought of that photograph in his bedroom, hidden in the desk drawer so Meg wouldn't see it. He wouldn't have kept it if he didn't care at least a little. She wouldn't have kept the pictures of him, either, or looked at them quite so often. Her life was a hopeless mess, and the only solution was to leave Brooktown as soon as the wedding was over.

Meanwhile there were still a few days to get in and a few inevitable meetings between them. She'd make a very determined effort to control her emotions. What else could she do? As her mind roved over the problem, Robyn lost sight of Sean and her sister. Jill had been right about the gloves. Her fingers were freezing, and she decided to go into the clubhouse for a cup of coffee.

Sean and Jill kept skating a little longer, but Jill noticed when Robyn left. "You didn't mention you were with your sister," Sean said.

"Didn't I?" Jill asked. "Well, I knew you didn't care about her." She took a surreptitious look from the corner of her eye and saw the grim set of Sean's lips. "Will Meg be mad?"

Not mad, he thought. Furious. "Don't be silly. Why should she? She had rehearsal tonight. She knows I don't like to go to her rehearsals."

"We loved your new house," Jill said, since he'd already mentioned the visit. "I was surprised to hear you're changing the bathroom. I don't think a modern Jacuzzi tub would look right in there."

"We're not changing the bathroom! What are you talking about?"

"Meg said she wanted a platform tub and a Jacuzzi. I guess you'd better consult with her before you do anything else, Sean. It's a shame you'll have to take that nice new blue covering off the stairs. If she's doing the living room in gold, though, she'll want gold carpet on the stairs, too."

Sean silently clenched his jaws, but didn't plan to tell Jill any tales she could carry back to her sister. "We haven't had much time to discuss the restorations yet. Meg's pretty busy with her play at the moment."

"Yes, and when that's over she'll be raising money for the permanent home for the dramatic society. You're probably relieved about that. I mean, you wouldn't want them having their rehearsals in your house for long once you're married."

Sean felt out of place with Meg's artistic friends. He was vaguely relieved that they took up so much of her time, but he didn't intend to have them cluttering up his house once he was married and living in it. He fell silent, and Jill didn't prod him for an answer. She'd given him something to think about.

"What do you say we stop and have a drink?" she suggested. "My toes are like ice."

"That's not a bad idea," he agreed, and pulled over to the edge of the rink.

There were half a dozen rough-hewn tables in the clubhouse. Robyn sat alone at one of them. Jill's scanning eye soon spotted her. "Shall we join Robyn?" she asked nonchalantly when Sean handed her the coffee. She headed in her sister's direction.

When she saw them, Robyn's heart gave the lurch that was becoming painfully familiar. She dreaded to confront Sean again, yet she was disappointed when he stopped to talk to one of his hockey players. But at least it gave her an opportunity to study him.

His face was highly colored from the wind and cold. A shock of blue-black hair fell over his forehead. She wanted to push it back. Sean had such soft, silky hair for a man. It was ruler straight. He always wore it cut short, like a businessman's. She'd talked him into the longer sideburns that he still wore. At this time of night, Sean usually had the beginning of a shadow around his jaw, unless he shaved again before a date. He hadn't shaved tonight, she noticed.

That beard would prickle Meg's tender skin if he was going to pick her up after her rehearsal. She pictured them kissing in the front seat of his car. He'd hold her close to keep out the cold. Robyn shook away the unwelcome image. Don't look at his face. Forget his eyes, which glowed like dark sapphires in the shadowy half-light. She looked away but felt her gaze drawn irresistibly back to him.

Sean didn't need the bulk of his fleece-lined jacket to pad his shoulders. She remembered their broad and strong contour. She knew how they felt, all warm and cozy in a sweater. And she knew the feel of them bare from when they used to swim, his body heated by the sun, his shoulders smooth as satin and hard as steel. His muscles were long and lean and hard, like an athlete's, not all knotty and bunched like a weight lifter's. As she watched, Sean reached out and gave the hockey player's shoulder a tap. Then he came to their table.

Robyn felt a nearly unbearable tension and was relieved when Jill spoke up. "Why didn't you invite Harry to join us?" she asked. "I'm dying to meet him.

He's a senior,'' she added with an air of importance. Robyn assumed Harry was the hockey player Sean had been talking to.

''He's too fast for you, child,'' Sean warned. ''But not on the ice, unfortunately. I've just been advising him to practice his speed skating.''

Jill pounced. ''When? I'll get Norma McIntyre to come to the rink with me.''

Sean gave a laughing look at Robyn before he turned to Jill. ''Where did you learn such cunning strategies, running after a man in that shameless fashion? Next you'll be going to his house.''

Robyn gave him a fulminating look that acknowledged the gibe and threatened retaliation. Her good intentions of acting calm began to dwindle.

''He doesn't live in a house,'' Jill said. ''He lives in an apartment. And there's no point in walking past it. He lives on the fifth floor at the back. When's he going to practice, Sean?''

''He mentioned Sunday morning, since the rink will be crowded in the afternoon.''

''Great! I've got to tell Norma,'' Jill said, and hopped up, leaving Robyn and Sean alone.

''Don't encourage her,'' Robyn said.

''This isn't the Dark Ages, Rob. Women don't need encouragement.'' A playful smile lifted his lips.

''I already told you. If you've taken the misguided idea I was running after you when I took Meg to your house, you're very much mistaken.''

A glint of mischief flashed in Sean's dark eyes. ''Don't disillusion me. I've never had women fight over me before. I think I like it. May the best woman win.''

"Fight over you?" Robyn was ready to say a lot more, but she saw his smile and realized he was goading her.

"I'm going to be the best man. Don't I deserve the best woman?" he asked reasonably.

Robyn lifted her chin in mock vanity and said, "The very best, Sean, and for that one occasion when you're the best man, you'll have her. Me! I'm the bridesmaid, remember?"

"How could I forget? If you're as good as you threaten, maybe I'll let you be my bridesmaid when I marry Meg."

"I don't do crowd scenes. Do you expect me to make a special trip to Brooktown just to be one of your six bridesmaids?" Now why did he give her that strange look? Good Lord, was it possible Sean didn't even know the elaborate plans Meg was making for the wedding?

"But you said you were moving back permanently," he said.

Robyn realized she had misread him. It was her involuntary speech about having to make a special trip that caught his interest. It was difficult to interpret his expression. Was he relieved? That question in his eyes suggested more curiosity than relief.

"I said Ed wanted me to," she pointed out, but in some confusion.

"You said, and I quote, 'It's my decision. I've decided to come back.' But then I shouldn't have taken you at your word. You were always good at changing your mind," he taunted.

She had no trouble reading his mood now. Sean's eyes smoldered with banked anger. Her staying in or leaving Brooktown couldn't upset him this much. Robyn knew instinctively that his anger was three years old. It was her decision not to marry him that caused those blue sparks to burn so angrily. Three years and he was still fuming. As though it weren't at least half his fault. As though he weren't the one who put the announcement in the paper!

"It's a woman's prerogative. I thought even you might have heard about it," Robyn said loftily, but she felt a quaking inside. If she wasn't careful, they'd have another fight, right here in front of half the high-school population.

"Heard about it? I learned that lesson firsthand, the way I learned everything else, at the school of hard knocks." His accusing stare sent Robyn's adrenaline gushing. A show of boredom seemed the likeliest way to defuse his anger.

"Oh, please! Let's not hear the blue-collar blues again," she said. "They don't teach disappointment at Harvard, Sean. We all have to learn to live with rejection in the real world."

His reply was swift and angry and instinctive. "What would you know about rejection?"

"Maybe I know a lot more than you think," she shot back. "I attended a few classes at the university of hard knocks myself." Her accusing glare reminded him of his part in her education.

A sudden hush had fallen over the room. A few heads turned to watch the squabbling couple. Sean never knew enough to keep his voice down. He might think of himself as a poor boy who made good, but his indifference to people's reaction had an aristocratic disdain.

"And please don't shout," Robyn added quietly. "People are starting to stare."

"I don't shout. I just raise my voice a little."

"No doubt that's why people are staring."

"Let them," he growled.

Robyn knew even while she was saying the words that they were unwise, but Sean could always make her lose control. Her only concession to decency was that she spoke in a low voice.

"Sure, let them stare. You'd enjoy that. You should join the dramatic society yourself. Jump up on the stage with Meg and let the whole town gawk at you. Then you'd be happy."

With an effort Sean, too, lowered his voice. "You can't leave Meg out of this, can you, Robyn? This is what it's all about. It really bugs you that I didn't go crawling after you and beg you to come back. I fell in love with a prettier woman instead, and I'm going to marry her."

"Go ahead! What do I care who you marry?" she asked with a fine show of indifference. "You could bribe anyone with that show-off mansion and diamond ring the size of a skating rink."

"I could afford to bribe a woman now, but in Meg's case, it wasn't necessary," he replied with a darkly accusing look. "She loves me for myself."

And Robyn didn't—that's what he meant. She wouldn't marry him because he wouldn't buy the house. But if he thought Meg would have him without the mansion, he was probably wrong. Robyn longed to tell him her impression of Meg but bit it back, because it would only sound like spite.

"I wasn't going with Meg when I bought the house," he said. "I bought it as a reward for myself."

"I hope you enjoy it."

"You won't be here to see whether I do or not. You're running away—again. What made you change your mind? Other than the fact that you're a woman, I mean?" he goaded.

"I have my reasons."

Behind Sean's narrowed eyes, a question shone. "You managed to bring old Jeff around your thumb, did you? He finally popped the question?" His voice was hard.

"You seem unduly interested in my marrying Jeff." Robyn smiled.

"I'd like to think you'll be sharing marital bliss, along with the rest of us. Ed and Noreen, Meg and me...."

He was just taunting her. She would *not* let him see how well he was succeeding. She would answer calmly and politely. Robyn gave a smile that would freeze the sun and said, "When I get engaged, you'll read it in the papers. Meanwhile don't hold your breath. And don't worry about me."

Sean stared so hard and so long that she felt she was being hypnotized by the concentration of his look. But when he finally spoke, his voice was void of emotion. Sean always used that cold tone when he was trying to hide his feelings. "Are you marrying the guy, or not?"

"No," she said calmly, and watched as a mask of frustration seized his features.

"Why not?"

"Because I don't love him."

"Did I get the name wrong? Is there somebody else?"

The blazing intensity of his look hadn't lessened. Robyn knew how desperate he was to know her answer, and despite his cold voice, she had a very good idea of why he wanted to know. Just what good it would do to satisfy him, however, was unclear. Sean was engaged, and there wasn't a chance in a thousand that Meg would let him off the hook. Why complicate so many lives? Sean must have loved Meg enough to propose to her.

"Not at the moment. Right now I'm concentrating on my career. If I ever meet a man I can't live without, I'll marry him—if he wants me."

"You do that," Sean said. His voice was gentle. It was his kiss-and-make-up voice, the anger all spent. "Don't let him get away, or you'll be sorry."

It was all he could say, and it was enough. Robyn understood him as well as if he'd admitted he still loved her. A man didn't flare up like lightning about someone he wasn't deeply involved with. His anger was the other side of love. If he didn't care, he'd be indifferent. There was no indifference in Sean's manner to her or her feelings about him.

Robyn felt tears gathering behind her eyes and knew she had to get away. "I'll remember that," she said, trying for a light touch. "Would you mind finding Jill for me? I'm ready for home."

"Sure," he said, and rose. But he didn't leave. He stood a moment, as though uncertain. "About that announcement in the paper, Rob. Did you ever discuss it with Ed?" Robyn frowned, trying to remember. "Maybe you should," he suggested, and left. Robyn sat on alone, pondering his speech.

In a minute Jill came alone to the table. "Are you going home already? We just got here."

"I'm bushed, Jill."

"You go on, then. I'll walk home later. It's not far."

"Okay."

"Sean said to say goodbye. He's skating again."

Robyn gave her sister a stinging look. "Did you know Sean was going to be here tonight, Jill?"

"How could I know? I just bumped into him when we got here, and asked him to skate with me."

"Why are you biting your lip?"

Jill hastily released her lip. "I think I'm getting chapped lips. It's the cold wind on my braces that causes it. Have you got anything to put on them?"

"I don't think you're telling the truth. If you've mounted some stupid campaign to bring us back together, Jill, I want it to stop. Now! You understand?"

Jill gave a blank look. "I don't know what you're talking about. How could you possibly get Sean back? He's marrying Meg. Even if he doesn't love her," she added with a melodramatic sigh.

"Of course he loves her."

"Do you think so? He isn't very happy about that Jacuzzi."

"You shouldn't have mentioned it. It's none of your business, Jill."

"I don't want him to make a mistake. I like Sean. I think somebody should tell him Meg isn't right for him. To tell the truth," Jill said doubtfully, "I feel kind of responsible."

Robyn gave a start of interest. "What do you mean? What did you do?"

Jill moved a little farther away. "I told him at Christmas that I thought you and Jeff would probably be getting engaged. I thought he'd give you a ring. I really *did*, Rob. You'd been writing about Jeff for months."

"I was only out with him half a dozen times!"

"Well," Jill said, scraping the blade of her skate along the floor, "I thought it was serious. I just happened to mention it to Sean, and right away he thought it was all settled. And the next day he got engaged to Meg—on the rebound. If he couldn't have you, he didn't want everybody feeling sorry for him. You know how proud he is."

"You're imagining things," Robyn said coldly. "His engagement has nothing to do with me. In any case I want you to butt out of it."

Robyn just wanted to be alone. She changed into her boots and carried her skates to the car. The windows were starred with frost crystals, and the vinyl seat was like ice. Her breaths made little clouds in the air. It had been a terrible idea to come here. Jill knew Sean would be here, too. She was apparently in hot pursuit of Harry. She must have known Sean was coaching the team.

When Robyn got home, she had to sit and talk to Ed and Noreen for half an hour before she could politely get away. When Ed went to the kitchen to make coffee, she followed him.

"Ed about that announcement Sean put in the paper when we broke up..."

Ed nodded his head, smiling. "Yeah, he told you about that?"

"He suggested I ask you."

"Then I guess it's all right to tell you. I'm afraid I led him astray there. I really thought that would make you think twice about breaking up." Ed was preparing the coffee, not taking much notice of his sister.

"*You* suggested it!" Robyn gasped.

"We were having a bull session one of the nights he came and you wouldn't see him," Ed admitted. "I told him drastic measures were called for. He was desperate to at least *see* you. He thought he could talk you around. I said you'd see him all right if he put that announcement in the paper. You'd knock his head off. Sean said, 'No, she won't. She'll be too happy that I'm going to take the job with Britten.' Then he gave kind of a bitter laugh."

He'd been ready to do that for her! Robyn felt like a Judas. "Oh, Ed, I wish you'd told me!"

Ed looked mildly surprised. "I wanted to, Rob. But you really didn't seem to give a damn by that time. You were all hot to go to Syracuse, and, well, you were kind of young to be getting married. Sean wasn't exactly in a position to set up house, either. It seemed best to let you simmer down." He poured cream and looked around for the sugar bowl.

"I've had three years to simmer down. Why didn't you tell me?"

"I asked Sean if he wanted me to. He forbade it. Pride, you know. I guess he didn't want you to know he'd capitulated. How come you two got talking about that?" Ed asked, merely curious. He had no idea of the havoc he'd created.

"We met at the rink tonight."

The coffee was ready. "Want some?" he asked.

"No, I think I'll go up to bed," Robyn replied, like one in a daze. She said good-night to Noreen and went upstairs.

It was all a mistake, a stupid misunderstanding. Sean had put the notice in the paper because Ed said it would make her see the light. Naturally Sean had believed him. Ed was her own brother, older and presumably wiser. But most of all she remembered that he'd been willing to take the job with Britten, much as he disliked it. He'd have altered the whole course of his career for the worse, for her.

She was almost glad he hadn't. Sean wouldn't have been happy, and that would have saddened her. If only she'd seen him. Sean would have offered to take the job, and she wouldn't have let him. It was just a token of his willingness, that's all she had really wanted. And now it was too late.

Tomorrow was Friday, the day of the wedding rehearsal and the party at Noreen's house after. Although Meg would probably attend just the party, Sean would be at both affairs. Another wretched evening. Then the wedding. And on Monday she could leave. She was sorry she'd told her mother she had Monday off. Mom expected her to stay the extra day.

Two more days. She could stand anything for two days, even this nagging ache in her heart. Sean had proposed to Meg only because he thought Robyn was going to marry Jeff Perkins. Jill was right about one thing. That was exactly the hotheaded, dumb, Irish thing Sean would do. Robyn could almost repeat what he'd said to himself. "I'll show her. She thinks I'm going to sit around, brokenhearted. I'll get engaged to the prettiest girl in town.''

He was always too hot at hand. Every time they had a fight, he did something stupid. Usually he asked out some girl he knew she didn't like. He made sure he went where she'd see him, too. It was all his insecurity, this showing her that other women liked him. But that was adolescent behavior. If Sean didn't have any more sense than that ... The logical corollary didn't follow. She still loved him. It was love that made him act so stupid. She was no better herself.

And it was hard to realize Sean still harbored insecurities, but it took time for a person to adjust to a new reality in his life. Sean hadn't grown up in a well-off home like hers. Some corner of his mind still felt that need to put on a good front. It was ironic, really. She thought Sean was so much better than most men. But he didn't think so. He didn't think he was good enough for her, so he'd propped up his self-doubts by asking Meg Britten to marry him, because she was prettier and richer.

The trouble was, Meg had said yes. And Meg wasn't the obliging sort to back out gracefully. Sean was exactly what she wanted. He'd make a stunning groom for her wedding show. She'd play house by adding modern monstrosities to an old, classical home.

Robyn lay down on her bed and closed her eyes. It would work out somehow. Things always did. Sean and Meg would arrive at some more or less compatible life-style. Maybe children would draw them together. Sean wanted two sons and a daughter. Robyn had wanted one son and two daughters. They couldn't even agree on that. What chance did they have of living peacefully together?

None. They wouldn't have lived peacefully. They would have squabbled like a pair of fishwives and been so very happy. In the unlikely case that fate was very kind and gave her another chance, Robyn felt she could do better. She was older now, more sensible. At least she'd know enough not to let him get away.

"Don't let him get away, or you'll be sorry," Sean had said. He had learned a lesson, too, now that it was too late.

Chapter Five

Friday was a hectic day at the Haltons' house, with last-minute preparations for the wedding on Saturday. Robyn volunteered to take over at the hotel in the afternoon so Ed could get his hair cut and attend to some wedding chores. She enjoyed the stint as acting manager. A few minor emergencies arose to enliven her afternoon. The weekly delivery of clean linen didn't arrive, and she spent half an hour on the phone pleading and threatening and finally tracking it down at the hospital.

One guest became quite drunk and disorderly in his room. Robyn knew that a hotel didn't call in the police unless absolutely necessary. That only offended the customer and gave the hotel a bad name. She sent two waiters upstairs to quiet the man and get him peacefully to bed to sleep it off.

Robyn wasn't at home when Sean Blake called to check on the hour of the wedding rehearsal that evening. It was Jill who answered the phone.

"I've forgotten whether it's at seven-thirty or eight," he explained.

Jill bit her bottom lip. "It's seven-thirty, Sean," she said, even before she formed a plan to capitalize on the misunderstanding.

Of course it was at eight, but if she could get Sean and Robyn to the church half an hour early... They'd be alone. They couldn't argue in church. The place would be decorated for a wedding, which was bound to put thoughts in their heads. Anything could happen in half an hour. Now all she had to do was arrange for Robyn to be there at seven-thirty, too.

When her mother returned from having her hair done, Jill began executing her scheme. "I hope they're decorating the church right for tomorrow," she said, shaking her head to show her doubt. "Noreen will be so disappointed if they forget to put the bows on the seats."

Mrs. Halton didn't seem very disturbed. "I doubt if she'd even notice the difference. Noreen isn't one to go in for a lot of pomp and ceremony."

"She was really interested in the flowers, though," Jill pointed out. "She wanted white mums mixed in with the poinsettias that are left over from Christmas."

"I'm sure everything will be fine," her mother said. "If you're that concerned, why don't you go over and check it out for yourself, dear?"

"They wouldn't listen to a kid. Robyn should go."

"Robyn has her hands more than full today, working at the hotel."

"I bet she'd be glad to do it," Jill said, and put on her coat to go down to the hotel.

Once there, Jill twisted the story just enough to make Robyn feel she should look into it. "Mom's worried they'll make a botch of the decorations. Do you think you could get away from the hotel half an hour early and go to the church at seven-thirty, Rob?"

"My replacement doesn't arrive till seven. I have to change after that. I'm going from the rehearsal to Noreen's party. I can't leave the hotel without a manager."

"Call the replacement and see if he can come in earlier."

"Well, if he can then I guess that would be all right."

When Jill left she congratulated herself that she'd managed the whole affair with only one real lie. Noreen *had* mentioned once that she hoped the church remembered the white mums. Mom hadn't objected when she said Robyn should go and check it out. She'd only lied to Sean, and anybody could make a mistake of half an hour, especially at a confusing time like this.

Although Robyn meant to keep a close eye on Jill, it never occurred to her that her sister would try to pull off one of her stunts at a church. When she went to the unoccupied suite on the top floor to dress for the rehearsal and party, Jill was the farthest thing from her mind. She thought of the busy afternoon and how much she'd enjoyed it. It was a good feeling, being in complete control, instead of having to check with a superior before making any decision.

At the moment Ed was actually the manager, but he trusted her implicitly. The arrangement was such that if she came home, he'd handle the accounting and finances, and she'd run the hotel on a day-to-day basis. Ed had no formal training in hotel management. He wasn't making maximum use of the convention trade, for instance. With the expanded facilities they could now handle small conventions. She had some ideas about starting an elegant Sunday brunch, too. People liked to go out to lunch after church on Sunday. The brunch in Syracuse was a big success.

But when Robyn finally left the shower to get dressed, she found her mind running straight back to Sean. He'd be at the rehearsal. At eight o'clock tonight, she'd be standing with him at the altar. Instead of a white gown, she'd be wearing the black sheath and glittering gold jacket that lent it style and color. Noreen's party tonight was the second-biggest do of the wedding festivities, and a fancy dress was definitely required.

The vanity and mirrors had been installed in the bathroom upstairs, and Robyn fixed her hair there. She brushed it back from her face and held it in place with the pretty gold combs Ed had given her for Christmas. The simple hairdo highlighted the contours of her face. A friend in Syracuse had said she'd kill for Robyn's high cheekbones that tapered to hollows at the back of her jaws. It wasn't a bad face, Robyn decided modestly, but tonight it looked sad. It was the eyes that did it. Shadows turned her amber eyes to a deep brown.

Or was it the sulky pout of her lips that made her look so dissatisfied? There was no use sulking. What's past is prologue, but it didn't seem right that one stupid, childish argument should have such disastrous and permanent results. As in a Greek tragedy, it wasn't just the argument, it was the character flaws that had caused this outcome. Foolish pride had caused Sean's heart to take offense too quickly, and Robyn had been too proud to hear his reasons.

She had always silently maintained that if he loved her, he'd do anything for her. That's what love was all about, wasn't it? And now she knew that he'd been willing to change. If only she'd learned it then. She should have been willing to do anything for him as well. She'd hurt herself, but what was even worse, she'd hurt the man she loved. Alone with her guilt and regrets, Robyn admitted she would have been a hundred times happier in an apartment with Sean than she'd been without him in Syracuse for the past three years.

And if she came back, she'd be without him in Brooktown, with the added irritation of seeing him with Meg. She couldn't face it. Accepting the inevitable didn't become easier with time. She'd have to tell Ed her decision before the wedding. It would be the hardest thing she had ever had to tell him. He was counting on her. And what excuse could she give? The only ray of consolation was that she knew Sean had truly loved her, and a part of him still did.

With a weary sigh, Robyn put on her boots, and her black fur-collared coat, picked up her purse and shoes and left.

No one was in the church except the organist, who was practicing the wedding hymns in the choir. The rich, solemn music rolled from the choir loft, filling the empty space below. Robyn checked that the ribbons were on the seats and the flowers arranged as Noreen wanted them. Everything was fine. The carved oak altar looked lovely with the white and red flowers. Festive, but still solemn, as a church should look. She was here half an hour early for no reason. There wasn't time to go home or back to the hotel, yet half an hour seemed a long time to sit alone. She went to the back seat and hunched down to think.

When Sean arrived at the church five minutes later, he recognized Robyn's car immediately. A quick look around the lot soon told him that the other members of the wedding party hadn't arrived yet. He wore a wary look when he went into the church, but he was reassured by the organ music. The car probably belonged to the organist. It wasn't an unusual make.

Sean didn't see Robyn at first. Her black coat and dark hair disappeared in the shadows. He walked slowly up the aisle, gazing toward the altar. He thought a church decorated for a wedding was a beautiful sight. With the golden notes from the organ swelling around him, he felt a choking sensation in his throat. Next June he and Meg would be standing at that altar, exchanging vows of eternal love, when he already knew his first fascination with her had faded to indifference.

Meg Britten no more loved him than she loved her Mercedes or his grandiose house. A house bought to appease another woman, to make up to Robyn for the little brick house he hadn't been able to buy her before. Robyn—that's who he should be walking down this aisle with. And what could he do about it? His engagement had been formally announced in the newspaper. Meg wore his engagement ring. Meg, apparently, already had elaborate plans underway for a wedding of enormous proportions.

It was a travesty. Ed and Noreen, truly and deeply in love, were having a small, family wedding. They'd even talked about being married at city hall, but their parents wanted some ceremony. It seemed the less substance the marriage, the more ritual and show were required to legitimize it.

There was nothing Meg liked better than a show. She wouldn't give up her role as Bride without a fight. And what could he do, he asked himself again. Whatever Meg's shortcomings, she didn't deserve to be cast aside like an old shoe because he decided he wanted to marry somebody else. He was far from certain that Robyn would accept him, anyway. Did she feel any of this desperate regret and longing that bedeviled him?

He wondered if he had ever really known her. He'd been so sure she'd come to harangue him about that announcement he put in the newspaper when they broke up. Robyn had a cold side to her. She had the fortitude to just walk away without a backward look. He couldn't have done that. She must never have loved him as much as he loved her. That was the crux of the whole matter.

While Sean stood at the altar thinking his private thoughts, Robyn cast a furtive glance at the door, wondering if she could escape without being seen. What was Sean doing here so early? Her heart thudded heavily. He couldn't possibly have known she'd be here. It was just a whim of fate that threw them together for their mutual torture. She couldn't blame Jill for this.

Since Sean hadn't seen her when he came in, he might overlook her if she sat very still. She hunched lower on the bench, hidden behind a pillar. Sean turned and began walking down the aisle. His head was bent, and a wistful, pensive frown drew his brows together. When Sean got to the back of the church, he turned and sat down in the back row with his head hunched into his collar. His reasons were similar to Robyn's: it was too late to go home, so he'd just sit here and wait and think.

That strange sixth sense that tells people they aren't alone caused him to look in Robyn's direction. Sean almost felt he was seeing an apparition. He'd been thinking of her, and there she was, her tantalizing face appearing from the shadows. Then he noticed she was wearing a peculiarly self-conscious expression.

"You're early," she whispered across the space. "The rehearsal isn't till eight."

"What are you doing here?" he demanded. Surprise lent a harsh edge to his words, but it didn't fool her.

"That's *my* line. Mom wanted me to come and check out the decorations. What's your excuse?"

Sean slid over closer to her, to avoid talking loudly. "Jill told me the rehearsal was at seven-thirty."

"Jill!" she exclaimed. She might have known! That child was going to have her neck wrung before the weekend was over.

"I wasn't sure of the time, and called. I got Jill."

"I see."

Sean knew that Robyn was angry. The sudden tightening of her facial muscles, and particularly the glitter in her amber eyes, told him so. From knowing her so well in the past, he knew the anger wasn't directed at him. He was beginning to have his own suspicions regarding Jill Halton. She had a sly way of peering from the corner of her eye when she talked to him. Why had she told him about Meg wanting the Jacuzzi, for instance?

"Did she call you, too?" he asked.

"She came in person to tell me about 'Mom's' request."

Sean gave a reluctant grin. "It seems we have an unwanted matchmaker on our hands. I wondered last night, when you turned up at the rink where I give my hockey team a workout."

"Next time I'll be on my guard."

"I feel like a sinner, talking in church. Shall we go into the hall?" Sean suggested.

The large hall attached to the side of the church was used for various meetings and bazaars and the semi-annual rummage sale. A short while ago, it had been the scene of the Christmas tea. Long tables were still arranged around the edge of the room and down the center. They went in and Sean removed his coat.

Beneath it a well-tailored dark jacket defined his broad shoulders and chest. The white shirt and discreetly striped tie made Sean look older, more authoritative and prosperous. The hotheaded young man she'd left in a fit of pique had matured into the epitome of the successful businessman. His camel-hair coat, thrown casually over one of the chairs, wasn't the kind the old Sean would have owned. Perhaps she was wrong to think he looked his best in casual clothes. There was a new air of assurance about him.

His kind of good looks wouldn't fade with youth. His strong features would go on improving with age. His dark eyes would assume wisdom and tolerance as life buffeted him. His face would become a little craggy, but his strong jaw would retain the firm perfection of young manhood.

"If she keeps this up, things could become a little embarrassing. You should speak to her," Sean said.

"Don't worry. I intend to."

"I wonder where she got this bee in her bonnet that we should be thrown together," he said, and gave her a long, questioning look. Sean's thirst to know how Robyn felt about him was becoming a mania. And something in her tentative, questioning look made him hope, in spite of common sense, that Robyn was instrumental in Jill's tactics.

"Youth is the time of romance. Romance and misunderstanding go hand in hand, Sean."

"Tell me about it." The trite words, which Sean uttered at random to hide his feelings, hung in the air, assuming meaning and importance from the past. Their eyes met in a question that firmed to knowledge. It was all a misunderstanding. The air was still, supercharged—like the atmosphere before a violent storm.

Robyn felt as if she were waiting for the roar of thunder and the flash of lightning that would clear away the old misunderstanding. But what good would it do? It would only increase the hurt.

"Anyway, we mustn't encourage her," Sean said.

"The only encouragement I gave her was to say I don't hate you. I don't know where you got the idea I do. That's why I smiled at you at the party. I didn't want you to think I hate you, Sean.'' Her tone held a reproach.

Hate was hardly the word Sean expected to hear. He looked first surprised, then disappointed. ''Hate me!'' But as he got control of himself, he added more mildly, ''That's a relief. I doubt if Plato would agree with hatred among friends.''

''You know what I mean. There's—nothing between us any longer,'' she said curtly, to hide her pain.

A satiric smile pulled his lips. ''Jill told me you dissolved in tears when you heard I was going to marry Meg. You yearned for one last dance with me! I asked you because I felt sorry for you.''

Robyn was momentarily speechless. What she had so blithely taken for unrequited love was just pity. The ignominy of having Sean feel sorry for her was too much to bear. Pity was the last resource of the rejected. But she would not shout. She made a conscious effort to keep her voice low when she answered.

''And you believed a story like that?'' She tried to sound amused, but her voice was colored with anger.

''Old gullible Blake.'' He smiled to show her he understood her feelings.

''How would you like to buy the Brooklyn Bridge? Everybody knows witches can't cry,'' she joked.

Nothing. No feelings. The woman was heartless. ''That's because they don't have a heart,'' he said. ''You've got to have heart, Rob. Don't you ever listen to the old show tunes?''

She welcomed the diversion. Banter was better than bawling, and that's what she felt like doing. ''Sure, the lyricists have to have something to rhyme with 'part.' I'll have you know I cried buckets when my spaniel died. And before you think I'm putting you down, I'm not comparing you to a mutt."

"Of course not. You loved your spaniel," he added with a sardonic look. "One thing about you intrigues me."

"Just one? Gee, I must be slipping."

"Maybe I should have said puzzled."

"No, stick with intrigue! I like it better."

"If you're not burdened with any feelings for me, why are you going back to Syracuse? It looks like a case of getting out of the kitchen because you can't stand the heat."

"What heat?" she asked.

"The heat of my marrying Meg Britten."

"That doesn't supply me with any heat. Just a warm glow of relief."

"I repeat my question. Why are you leaving town, then? Ed needs you at the hotel."

Robyn lifted an arched brow. "Why are *you* hinting I should stay? Yesterday you ordered me to leave."

"That should have ensured your staying. Don't leave on my account. It doesn't make any difference to me." The last words nearly choked his throat. To hide his discomfiture, Sean glanced at his watch, then toward the doorway.

This suggestion that he was becoming bored angered Robyn. "This is a sudden turnaround, isn't it?" She stared at him till he was forced to meet her eyes.

"I overreacted when you hit me unexpectedly with the news. I just thought things might be a little embarrassing. Now that I've had time to think about it, I see that it doesn't really matter," he said coolly.

"Second thoughts, you mean?"

"Something like that, yeah. As you said, it was all over between us a long time ago."

"Then maybe it's time to get rid of my picture. Meg might not like it, if she happened to see it in your bedroom."

Robyn hadn't meant to mention the picture. She'd been touched that he kept it near him, but his ruthless denial of having any interest in her was enough to goad her into indiscretion.

"What picture?" Sean demanded. His mind made a hasty scramble over his bedroom. Did she mean the room at the new house where he occasionally did some work? She might have been there. She certainly hadn't been in his apartment bedroom, and that's where he kept her picture.

"The one Jill spotted when she was snooping upstairs at the new house."

"There's no picture of you there. It sounds like more conniving on Jill's part."

Robyn realized too late that Jill probably *had* been lying. She was letting hope color her perceptions again. "My mistake. You're probably right. We'll blame this one on Jill," she said, calming down. "If she invites me on any more outings, I'll refuse. I don't know where she got the misguided idea that you and I should—"

Sean waved it away. Now that he'd won his point, he was half-sorry. He was also curious. "So you weren't surprised at all when you heard about Meg and me?" he asked, pulling out a chair and sitting across from Robyn.

She was uncomfortable with his face so close to hers. He looked at her with the keenest interest gleaming in his navy-blue eyes. She remembered every line and angle of his face. She loved the way his black hair grew around his temples. The memory of her fingers playing in it provided a nearly irresistible temptation.

"A little," she admitted. Her voice was flat with the effort of controlling her emotions. "I didn't dissolve in tears. It's time you were settling down," she said nonchalantly. *Oh, but you should be settling down with me!* "It was rather sudden, though, wasn't it?"

"I didn't see any point in waiting. We aren't getting any younger."

Robyn nodded and a silence fell. Sean wondered if she knew why he'd proposed to Meg. He didn't intend to tell her; his healthy pride prevented that final indignity. He'd rather suffer in silence. At least he didn't have to worry that Robyn was suffering, too. That would have been too much to bear.

Jill had completely fooled him on that score. How quickly he'd taken it for the truth, because in his deepest heart he wanted so much to believe Rob still loved him. Her not marrying Jeff had given Sean pause, but not loving Jeff didn't mean she loved him. She was genuinely angry with her sister.

Actually, Sean found Jill's concern rather touching. Of course he had to complain for the looks of it, but he certainly bore Jill no ill will for her efforts at reconciling him with Robyn. He scanned his mind for a harmless topic to pass the remaining minutes till the others arrived and said, "I hope the couple have good weather tomorrow."

"The forecast said clear and cold. That means their flight to the Bahamas should be able to take off on time."

"That's good. And they'll appreciate the heat all the more, after the chill here. It would be nice to get away from the cold for a while."

Sean felt self-conscious after he'd made that speech. To his ears, sensitive to double meanings, it seemed to refer to his own life without Robyn. Even these few private moments in her company were good. She looked regal, with that big black fur collar brushing her chin. Robyn was a proud, haughty, high-spirited woman. The kind of woman a man wouldn't tire of easily. Even after being engaged to her, he was never quite sure how she'd react to things.

"I wouldn't have chosen the Bahamas myself," Robyn said.

"You always wanted to go to Mexico."

It was one of the endless subjects that had fueled their discussions in the past. When they had talked about their first trip together, it was their honeymoon that they had meant. "And you wanted to go to Greece to see the old Grecian ruins," Robyn said. A wistful note crept into her voice.

"I went to Greece last winter." *But it wasn't much fun without you.* The Parthenon by moonlight, the amphitheater where he'd wanted to stand down at the bottom and tell Robyn he loved her. You could hear a whisper from the old stage, way up in the bleachers.

"Did you like it?"

"It was magnificent. The cradle of Western civilization. For me that means classical architecture. It was all I hoped for and more,'' he said with hearty enthusiasm that rang hollow to his own ears.

"I went to Rome last summer.'' *And thought of you when I looked at all the old, shattered buildings.* "You really should go to Rome next.''

They talked awhile about their holidays. At five to eight, the church door opened and they heard Ed's voice in the vestibule.

"Here they are, at last!'' Robyn exclaimed with a smile of relief. Yet she wasn't entirely happy the brief private meeting was over.

"Just when we were getting along so well.'' Sean smiled. "Do you realize we've been talking for half an hour without arguing?''

"We didn't *always* fight!'' Robyn objected. She didn't want him to remember only the arguments. There had been the good times, too. Wonderful times. Arguing was just the spice in the pudding.

"That's true. We always made up in fine fashion, didn't we, Rob?'' he said lightly. Then he picked up his coat, and she followed him to the door to meet the new arrivals.

There was a general melee as Robyn assured her mother and Noreen that the decorations were all in place. She spotted Jill, hanging back guiltily. "I'll speak to you later, young lady,'' she said in a low voice.

Jill gave a wide-eyed, innocent look. "What's that supposed to mean?''

"You know perfectly well! You sent Sean here early.''

"Oh, gosh! I forgot! I told him seven-thirty, didn't I? I thought the rehearsal was at seven-thirty. You just ask Mom. I was all dressed in my coat and everything at seven-thirty. It was too late to phone Sean then and tell him.''

Mrs. Halton asked Jill to go and tell the minister they were waiting, and Jill was glad for an excuse to escape. An impish smile curved her lips as she ran along the walk to the manse. There hadn't been a sound coming from the church hall when Ed opened the door. If she could get them together in an isolated spot for a couple of hours, she was sure they'd make up.

The rehearsal went forward with no major hitches. Robyn didn't experience the awful swell of desolation she had expected to when she stood at the altar with Sean. Her mind was too busy with other things. She had a strong feeling, however, that when they were dressed in their wedding finery tomorrow, with all the candles lighted and the minister saying the fateful words, she'd break down and bawl. That should please Sean. He seemed eager to see her cry.

After the rehearsal the throng went to their cars. Noreen was giving Sean last-minute directions to her house, as he'd never been there.

Jill, listening at Sean's elbow, said, ''Don't worry, Sean. Meg knows where it is. You're picking Meg up, aren't you?''

''No, she's coming over after the rehearsal.''

Jill caught her bottom lip between her teeth. That meant Meg would be driving her own car. Sean wouldn't be driving her home. Too bad Rob had driven her car. It shouldn't be hard to flatten a tire, though. Then she'd have to make sure Sean and Rob were the last ones to leave, so he'd have to drive her home. It was going to be a busy party.

Jill turned to follow her mother to their car. She felt a hand on her arm, holding her. Sean peered down and said, in a meaningful voice, "Why don't you drive over with me, Jill? You can show me the way. I have something I want to say to you."

"Oh—I—"

Sean began walking rather quickly toward his car. "All right," she agreed, since she couldn't break free and didn't want Robyn to see she was being forced.

Chapter Six

Jill felt completely grown up and very sophisticated when Sean held the car door for her. But when he got in and turned a dark eye on her, she suddenly felt about six years old.

"All right, brat, let's hear your story," he demanded.

"I'm sorry I sent you over to the church half an hour early, Sean. My mistake. I goofed. Now hadn't we better get going?" The others' cars were pulling out of the parking lot.

"It wasn't a mistake, Jill. You did it on purpose. You misinformed me—on purpose—about a couple of other things that have caused me a good deal of embarrassment, as well. I blame myself for believing that your hard-hearted sister ever shed a tear in her life, but when you told her I had her picture in my bedroom, you went too far."

"You mean she told you about that!" Jill wailed. "And I thought everything was going so well when the two of you weren't fighting tonight at church."

Sean hadn't the heart to go on upbraiding her. She looked too much like Robyn. He wished he'd known Robyn at this vulnerable age. He reached out and patted Jill's clenched hands.

"I appreciate your effort, Jill, but you're wasting your time. It's too late."

She gave a howl of protest. "It's not too late! You're not married yet, and Rob doesn't even have a boyfriend. I know she loves you, Sean."

"Then you know more than I do," he said with a rueful shake of his head.

"Of course I do. I'm her sister. Just because she clenches her jaw every time somebody mentions your name, it doesn't mean she doesn't love you. In fact it means she *does*," Jill explained with awful intensity. "It's all my fault that you got engaged to Meg. I only told you Jeff was proposing to Rob so you'd get busy and ask her yourself. And then you went and proposed to Meg," she wailed.

Sean was silent for a minute, wondering if he dared to believe her. If there was even a grain of truth in it... He wanted to emit an anguished wail of his own, but as that was impossible, he gave a lecture instead.

"You see the harm a lie can do, even a well-intentioned one. The one thing you can't fight is facts, Jill. The fact is I'm engaged to Meg, and I have to— I'm going to marry her," he said, silently cursing himself for the slip. "You'd be doing both Rob and me a favor if you stopped your little stunts."

Jill studied him in the shadows. "I don't think she's right for you, Sean. Meg should marry some millionaire that won't ask too much of her. Just to look beautiful and smile and spend his money."

"Meg's not like that," he felt obliged to say.

"Then how come the two of you never talk? She doesn't know anything about your work. She called it renovation. Even *I* know you do restorations. Why don't you—"

Sean's impatient look told her she had hit a nerve, but he cut her off abruptly. "I'm the one asking the questions and laying down a few laws, too. No more tricks. It's all over between Rob and me. I'm marrying Meg, period."

He hadn't said he loved Meg. Sean hated to tell a lie, but Jill had less aversion to one and said, "All right, Sean. I'm sorry. No more tricks. But I think you and Rob are making a terrible mistake."

"We all make mistakes. It's part of life. Show me a man who says he never made a mistake and I'll show you a grade A liar. Okay, lecture's over," he said, and turned the key in the engine. He immediately switched the conversation to his hockey team, knowing Harry Enfield would prove a distraction. There was no more lecture during the rest of the trip.

The party at Noreen's house was composed of friends and family of the couple. Except for a few out-of-town aunts and cousins, most of the attendees had known each other for years. They settled into groups to talk. Robyn moved from group to group, catching up on news and gossip. She noticed that Sean had no trouble mixing with the guests. He managed to make himself agreeable to the ones he hadn't known before. He was always a good mixer.

She was careful to keep half a room between them at all times, which didn't prevent her from looking. Her eyes seemed ineluctably drawn to Sean. His crow-black head stood out in the throng. The echo of his deep, masculine chuckle found her out, and she couldn't resist glancing at him. It was paltry behavior on her part, when Sean was doing such a magnificent job of ignoring her.

The evening dragged on. They arrived at the house at nine. At ten Meg still hadn't come from the play rehearsal. Robyn heard someone ask Sean if she was coming.

"She'll be here," he said confidently. "They often rehearse till midnight, but tonight she promised she'd break it off early."

It was a strange romance he was having with Meg, if she often rehearsed that late. They were just newly engaged. Robyn thought Sean would object to such cavalier treatment. He hadn't been so understanding when she was late for a date!

Robyn took one more look across the room and saw Sean stealing a glance at her. For one brief instant, their gazes locked. Then Sean looked away immediately, as though he'd been caught in an illegal act. It was as good as an admission that he still loved her. Why should he feel guilty for looking if it was only a disinterested glance?

But it hadn't been disinterested. It had been overflowing with emotion. There was rampaging interest in it. It was the kind of a look that would stay in her memory for years. It spoke of frustration and love that wouldn't be denied at least a look.

Robyn was overwhelmed. She felt tears gathering in her eyes and walked quickly to the kitchen. Even there she found no privacy. Noreen's mother was bustling about, uncovering plates of food. Robyn knew she should offer to help, but she wasn't up to it.

There was a playroom off the kitchen and down two stairs. It was unoccupied, lighted only by the lights from a small Christmas tree on a table.

"Mind if I have a look at the tree, Mrs. Crawley?" she asked.

"Go ahead, dear. It's only artificial, but we always had the tree in the playroom when the children were young. It wouldn't be Christmas without it."

"I know what you mean. At our house it's the crèche, even though the statues are all nicked."

Robyn went gratefully into the dark room and stood gazing silently at the tree. The lights appeared fuzzed around the edges, due to her unshed tears. The little synthetic tree looked quite beautiful when you didn't see it clearly. Life was like that, too. It looked good if you didn't examine it closely.

She was young, healthy and fairly attractive. She had a good job with a brilliant future, but she felt as lifeless as that plastic tree. What good were her youth and health and some beauty if they couldn't gain her the man she wanted? What pleasure was there in a brilliant career lived out away from her home and family and friends? What peace was there for her, knowing she had hurt Sean?

Robyn drew a long sigh and went to sit alone on the sofa. It was on the far side of the room, in deep shadows. At this angle she was cut off from a view of the kitchen. She'd just sit a minute and compose her thoughts before rejoining the party. She hadn't been there a minute when Sean's form reared up at the top of the two steps. He looked into the dark room, frowning, and Robyn knew he had followed her. He was looking for her. She sat perfectly still, hoping—and fearing—that he'd leave.

That look exchanged in the living room had found its way to Sean's heart, too. Jill said Rob still loved him, and he had to know if it was true. It wouldn't change things in any material way, but it would be some small consolation to know that she loved him.

He came down the two stairs and saw her huddling in the dark. Her glittering jacket sparkled with reflections from the colored lights, covering her in an evanescent shimmer. Robyn sat, waiting for some sarcastic comment that would put the fight back into her. She really needed a goad to prod her out of this somber mood.

"So this is where you've gotten to," Sean said in a gentle voice, and walked over to sit beside her.

He sensed her mood and softened his behavior accordingly. She'd nearly forgotten Sean had this gentle, considerate side.

"I was just admiring the tree," she said, trying for a normal tone.

"There's a bigger one in the living room."

"I like this one. It has memories," she said, and continued gazing at the fuzzed lights.

Was that a tear in the corner of her eye? Sean watched as she tried to blink it away. "Sad memories, to judge by your expression."

"Glad and sad. That's the way memories are, don't you think?" she asked, and turned her head to gaze at him. She saw love glowing in his eyes, and felt the same way Sean looked. All soft and melting inside with the haunting memories of their past love. No words were necessary. It was a tacit, mutual acknowledgement of their feelings.

Sean reached for her hand and squeezed it. "Maybe it's time to give up our memories, Rob."

She knew exactly what he meant by this oblique speech. *We're caught up in a bad situation of our own making, and what we must do is forget each other.* Easier said than done! A dozen angry, hurtful replies jumped to her mind, but she didn't give voice to any of them. Why deny the obvious?

She continued gazing at him. "I was just taking one last look." She looked long and hard at this man, who would soon be only a memory to her. She wanted to memorize him like this, with his features softened in a rueful smile. Black hair forming a graceful arc around his high forehead. Dark eyes gleaming with a sense of shared loss. Sensuous lips slightly open, with a glint of white teeth behind. Strong carved jaw that could so quickly harden to anger or soften in love.

"I'm sorry things turned out like this," he said. She had never heard Sean's voice so close to breaking. It almost undid her, but he spoke quickly, trying to establish a less emotional mood. "I spoke to Jill. I don't think we'll have any more tricks from that quarter."

"I spoke to her, too."

But even while they talked, his fingers tightened on hers till her hands ached. That one betraying gesture revealed his true feelings.

"I guess we shouldn't be too hard on her," he said. "She didn't mean any harm, you know."

"No." Robyn dared not risk another word till she got a grip on herself. Her voice was husky with unshed tears.

"Will you be leaving right after the wedding?"

"I have Monday off. I planned to leave Monday."

"I'm going to say goodbye now, Rob. We may not have another moment alone. I'm sorry I was so impossible about the house you wanted. I've regretted it a dozen—a hundred times. If you ever think of me in the future, try not to think too badly of me. You don't know how much I wanted to give you the house. But it seemed to me you wanted to marry the house and a safe job, not me. Do you understand what I'm saying?"

Robyn gazed into his troubled eyes. "Ed said—" She looked a question at him.

"I did tell Ed I'd take the job with Britten. To tell the whole truth, though, I planned to try to talk you out of it after we were married and you couldn't escape me."

"I wouldn't have held you to it," she replied. He was being completely sincere and honest, and she determined to return the compliment. "I thought you were just being your usual stubborn, Irish self."

"Maybe there was a little of that as well," he conceded.

"I guess we were too young then to think of anyone but ourselves. I was, anyway. You were right to stick to your guns. Your success proves it. You're doing beautiful work, Sean. It was wrong of me to try to change that. I never understood exactly what career plans you had.''

A glow of satisfaction flashed briefly over his face. Her praise was balm to his torn spirits. That was what he wanted to hear before they parted forever. How like Robyn to sense his need and fill it. And in the middle of his joy, the memory of future sorrow reared up. He answered lightly, to hide his pain.

''It sounds like a case of that twentieth-century bogeyman, a breakdown in communications. I shouldn't have allowed myself the luxury of anger when you said you were coming home. That was rude and unforgivable.''

Robyn swallowed the lump that kept growing in her throat. ''It's all right. You don't have to apologize anymore, Sean. Maybe you should go now, before—'' Before Meg's arrival. Meg wouldn't like finding Sean and Robyn alone in a dark room.

He shook his head and smiled. ''Don't worry. I have no intention of fighting with you tonight. I'm glad we had this talk. My conscience has been bothering me for the last three years or so. I've often wanted to call you.''

''Why didn't you?''

Sean gave a grin that tried manfully to make light of the hurt that gnawed at him. ''Because I'm too proud and stubborn. No crawling for me. I always preferred the grand gesture—'' He came to a quick stop.

The grand gesture—what did he mean by that? The Rinehart house! He *had* bought it for her! Having failed to give her the little brick cottage, he was making up by buying the mansion. She knew it as surely as if he'd told her in words.

He'd only bought the house this autumn. It confirmed that his sudden proposal to Meg was the work of a moment's anger. He'd meant to tell Robyn about the house when she came home for Christmas. He'd even installed her favorite color of carpet on the stairs. The breath caught in Robyn's throat at how much he loved her.

"Oh, Sean!" The words were out before she could stop them. They were a futile wail of protest against fate. She felt scalding tears gather in her eyes. One trickled slowly down her cheek.

Sean saw it and was wrenched inside. "Rob, don't..." His hands went out instinctively to comfort her. They touched her shoulders and closed tightly, possessively. He wanted so much to gather her in his arms and kiss away her tears. When he spoke his voice was husky with grief. "Don't cry over me. I'm not worth it, darling."

Robyn didn't trust herself to answer. Her bottom lip wobbled uncontrollably when he called her darling. He didn't even realize he'd said it. Sean took out his handkerchief and wiped at her tears with infinite tenderness. Her hands went to his chest, splayed over it while their eyes held, unblinking. She had to touch him. Just once.

She lifted her right hand and placed it on his cheek. He felt fevered. Sean's jaws quivered in an effort to endure the exquisite torture of her touch, but he didn't flinch, though his whole body pulsed with desire. His head slowly inclined closer to hers, and his gaze concentrated on her lips.

Just as it seemed he was losing control, Robyn reluctantly pulled her hand away. She'd caused this man too much grief already. Their meetings were agonizing for them both. She must say something to break the bewitching spell.

"See, I *do* know how to cry." She smiled through her tears. "I'm becoming pretty good at it."

Meg couldn't have timed her entrance more dramatically or more disastrously if she'd planned it. She appeared at the top of the stairs, outlined in a halo of light from the kitchen. "Sean!" she called. "Sean, darling! I'm here. Sorry I'm late."

Then she began walking down the stairs, carefully holding on to the railing because of her very high heels. Sean and Robyn exchanged a dismayed look. He jumped from the sofa and went forward to greet Meg.

"About time you got here," he said heartily, and gave her a peck on the cheek.

Meg's blond head moved to the side and she peered into the sofa corner. "Who's that with you, Sean?"

"Rob Halton," he said, and put a hand on Meg's elbow to lead her back upstairs, to give Robyn time to compose herself.

Meg planted her little feet flat on the floor and refused to budge. "What on earth were the two of you doing alone in the dark? As if I didn't know," she added with an angry little laugh.

She brushed Sean's hand away and walked purposefully toward Robyn. "A good try, Robyn, but it won't work. I suggest you quit making a fool of yourself," she said in a low but angry voice.

Robyn felt more guilty than angry. "We were just talking, Meg," she said in a controlled voice.

"I heard all about your chasing Sean down to the hockey rink. Did you have a nice talk there, too? You should have warned your sister not to tell tales."

Robyn winced to hear that Jill was still trying to make mischief. She was glad Sean couldn't hear them. Even as she thought this, he began to walk toward them. "It's a public rink, Meg. You're being paranoid," she said.

"Sean Blake is now my private property. I suggest you remember it." She turned angrily and went to meet Sean. "I see I'm going to have to keep a closer eye on you," she teased, trying to hide her ire. "That's what I get for being engaged to such a handsome man. Darling, you'll never guess what happened tonight at rehearsal."

Robyn sat alone, listening as Meg's voice receded into the distance. She felt like an idiot. Meg had behaved rather well, considering the provocation. You couldn't blame her for being jealous at finding her fiancé sitting in the dark with his ex-fiancée. That had really been indiscreet of her and Sean.

But there had been no real harm in it. She was glad she'd had that last private talk with him. She was gratified to know the house had been bought for her, even if it was Meg who would live in it. Robyn didn't even have the consolation of being able to despise the woman who had supplanted her. Meg had won Sean fair and square. The fault was their own, hers and Sean's, but mostly hers. They'd just have to deal with the consequences as best they could.

The first step was to rejoin the party and pretend nothing had happened. The second step would be to find Jill and blister her ears for telling Meg about the meeting at the skating rink. A cursory look around the room showed that Jill was missing. Robyn decided her younger sister must be in the washroom, but after five minutes Robyn became suspicious. She went down the hall toward the downstairs powder room and saw the door was open.

She checked in the closet. Jill's coat was gone. She went immediately and asked her mother where Jill was.

"Isn't she here?" Mrs. Halton asked, her eyes wide with alarm.

"Her coat's gone," Robyn said.

"Good gracious, where can she be? It's ten-thirty. She wouldn't have gone home without telling us."

Before they raised the alarm, Jill came back into the living room. The ruddy color of her cheeks and nose left no doubt that she'd been out. She hurried forward to explain her absence.

"It's so pretty outside I went for a little walk. Just up and down this street. Everybody's got their trees lighted up. The Stinsonses have a big wooden Santa Claus coming out of their chimney, with three reindeers on the roof. There should be eight."

This explanation sounded reasonable. Robyn had admired all the lighted trees when she drove to Noreen's house. Mrs. Crawley walked into the room with a platter of food, and Jill's disappearance was forgotten.

Robyn was careful to keep away from Sean and Meg. She didn't even let herself look at them, which was difficult as Meg had a way of garnering everyone's attention. To keep herself harmlessly occupied, Robyn helped serve the food and drinks. She overheard scraps of conversation. Meg was regaling the company with details of *Pygmalion*.

"Mr. Malcolm Auer from New York is coming to critique the play for us," she was telling some people from out of town. "The Brooktown Dramatic Society placed second in the state contest last year. That competition is held in Rochester. If we win we'll be entered in the Eastern amateur competition. It's held in New York. PBS will be filming."

"When is the competition?" someone asked.

"The New York State competition is in March. The Eastern competition is in June, I believe."

Jill adopted an innocent face and said, "Aren't you planning to be married in June, Meg?"

"The competition doesn't last a month," Meg pointed out. "And anyway, the wedding date isn't final. We can get married in May or July."

"You said you wanted a June wedding," Jill persisted.

Meg gave her a bright, angry little smile. "I may change my mind about that." She lifted her eyes and directed a long stare across the room at Robyn, then said, "January is beginning to look like a good month."

Robyn felt the message in that speech was aimed directly at her. It was a statement that Meg was taking no chance of losing Sean.

Jill's most recent plan of throwing her sister and Sean together failed. They weren't the last ones to leave the party. Robyn and her mother left a little early. When she discovered her flat tire, she simply drove home in the family car and called the garage to put on the spare and deliver the car to her house.

Robyn suspected Jill might have been instrumental in the flat, but she was too depressed to have it out that night. She went straight up to bed and lay awake thinking for a long time. The situation appeared hopeless, and her only consolation was that Sean still loved her, even if he was too much of a gentleman to say it. And she loved him so much she didn't know how she could face the future without him.

Since Sean was marrying Meg, the best she could hope for was that Meg truly loved him, and that Sean at least cared for Meg. In time he'd forget that he once loved Robyn Halton.

Chapter Seven

Although the wedding wasn't taking place till two o'clock, the Halton household was up at seven-thirty to begin preparations. Robyn had arranged with Ed to spend a few early hours at the hotel checking arrangements for the reception. She also had some instructions for Mr. Spence, who would act as manager during Ed's absence.

Ed went to the closet to help Robyn with her coat. "It will be a relief when you're back home to help out, Rob," he said. "I've been tied to the place so tightly. I can always have Jack Spence help out in a pinch, but he doesn't really know the business. Once I'm married it will be good to have a weekend off occasionally. How soon can you come home? You'll have to give a couple of weeks' notice at work, I suppose."

Robyn had put off telling Ed her decision. She didn't usually procrastinate. It was that hardy thing, hope, that caused the delay. She had gone on hoping, in spite of all, that somehow she and Sean could get back together.

But since they weren't going to, she had to tell Ed before he left on his honeymoon. This moment, though not good, was about the last chance she'd have. She regretted having to give him bad news just before his wedding. Ed needed her now, and it went against the grain to let him down. "I've decided not to come back after all, Ed," she said reluctantly.

When Ed recovered from shock, his face fell in disappointment. "Why not? It's the logical thing. You like Brooktown, don't you?"

"Of course I do. I love it. It's just that—" Words failed her. She couldn't think of a single credible excuse.

"I've been counting on you, Rob. Won't you reconsider?"

Robyn wanted very much to take the job. She was trying to convince herself that Sean and Meg would have a happy marriage, and that she could live with it. She just needed some time to get used to the idea.

"Maybe in the spring," she said. "The hotel in Syracuse is short staffed just now. When the spring graduates hit the market, they can probably replace me."

Ed noticed her distress and had an idea what had caused it. "It's Sean, isn't it?"

She shrugged her shoulders and didn't deny it. "I thought I could handle it. It seems I can't. Not yet."

Ed gave a resigned tsk. "It's a rotten shame. I just hope you don't do something foolish, like Sean...."

"Don't you think it will work out with him and Meg?" she asked anxiously. This made her decision even harder—the real conviction that Meg and Sean were ill suited.

Ed shrugged. "I suppose it will have to. It seems to me they rushed into the engagement without really getting to know each other. Sean won't treat her the way her parents have always done. She'll have to share him with his work."

"But she has her dramatics."

"That's a hobby, Rob. It only occupies her when a play's in rehearsal. Don't you go accepting any offers of marriage that will keep you away from Brooktown permanently."

"Don't worry, I won't. I've got to run now. If I don't have another chance, Ed, I want to wish you all the best. I know you and Noreen will be very, very happy." This was one thing that was going right, at least, and it caused one bright spot in Robyn's day.

"She's worlds too good for me," he said simply. "I don't think we could be unhappy if we tried, not as long as we've got each other."

His words left a bittersweet feeling in Robyn's heart as she drove to the hotel. That was exactly how she felt about Sean. She couldn't be unhappy with him, not if they were poor, not if his beautiful house fell in on their heads, not if the whole town despised them. As long as they had each other, they'd be happy living in a hut. And she knew instinctively that any one of those catastrophes would destroy Meg's married happiness.

* * *

Jill rose a little later than the others. At eight-thirty she came downstairs and sat alone at the table. She had failed in her plan, and her expression was sulky as she sat staring at the cornflakes box. If there was any excitement this morning, it would be at the hotel, and she decided to go down there. She could have bacon and eggs without the bother of making them.

When she reached the main street, she stopped at various stores to examine the after-Christmas sales advertised in the windows. Jill hardly bothered to glance in at Stolman's Clothing Store. Their idea of a sale was to reduce a sweater from $250 to $175. Nobody shopped there but stupid rich people. As she passed the door, it opened and Meg Britten came out, laden with bulging bags.

"Hi, Jill!" She smiled. "I thought you'd be busy this morning, getting ready for the wedding."

"I am ready. I decided to go and have breakfast at the hotel."

"I was just going to have a coffee myself. Why don't you join me? My treat," she said temptingly.

Jill noticed a curious gleam in Meg's eyes, and wondered why Meg should suddenly want to talk to her.

"Sure, thanks," she said, and went along.

When she had a cup of coffee and two hot Danish pastries before her, Jill said, "Are you all ready for the wedding, Meg?"

"Good heavens, no! I haven't even set the date."

What an egotist! Jill thought. "I meant Ed and Noreen's," she explained.

"Oh, that. Yes, I'm ready. I was wondering—since you know Sean so well—do you think he'd be very angry if I postponed our wedding till September?"

"I think he'd be furious," Jill said, and took a bite of her Danish. "Sean's nice, but he has an Irish temper."

"I seem to remember he and Robyn had some quarrels."

Jill smiled. "I hope you like fights. They used to argue about everything, but I guess that's the way it is when two people love each other. Things matter so much, I mean." A currant impaled itself on her braces and she tried to wiggle it off with her tongue.

"Yes," Meg said, and sipped her coffee. She and Sean had never argued. Not once. Why didn't Sean object to her rehearsals, for instance? She had a sinking feeling he'd object plenty if it was Robyn Halton he was engaged to.

Meg was being nice, and it made Jill feel guilty. So to make up for past wrongs, she said, "If you don't want to make Sean mad, I suggest—"

"But I *do*," Meg said with a certain force.

"Oh! Well in that case, all you have to do is delay the wedding. Or change the house to a modern style. Sean likes restorations, Meg, not renovations. He likes to keep the integrity of historical buildings. He was always talking about that when he expanded the hotel. Of course the expansion had to be modern, but he wanted to make it fit in with the older part."

Meg nodded. "I haven't actually discussed the redoing of the house with Sean. We're both so busy, you know."

"It must be fun, being an actress," Jill said with perfect sincerity.

They discussed this while Jill finished her pastries. Later Meg said in an offhand way, "Ed mentioned that Robyn's coming back to work in the Halton Hotel. When is she coming?''

"She isn't. She decided not to," Jill told her.

Meg's eyes flashed with interest. "Why is that?"

"I guess she prefers a bigger city."

Jill knew Meg didn't believe her and was relieved that she didn't ask any more questions. "I have to go now," Jill said, and got up. "Thanks for the breakfast, Meg. I'll see you at the wedding."

Meg stayed and had another cup of coffee. Her pretty face wore a determined expression as she stirred a package of noncaloric sweetener into her cup. She didn't want Robyn Halton to leave town. She wanted her to stay and try her damnedest to steal Sean away. That was the only way Meg would ever know for sure that Sean really loved her. She wouldn't give Sean up—not yet, anyway. First she'd put him to the test.

At three minutes to two the wedding party assembled in the vestibule of St. George's Church. A peep through the door showed Robyn that Ed and Sean were already making their way toward the altar to await the arrival of the bride. Noreen looked very pretty and as nervous as a brood hen. Two flags of red stood out on her cheeks, and her hands were trembling.

Robyn was nervous, too. The headband that had been too tight was now a little too loose. She had anchored it with bobby pins that dug into her scalp and would certainly cause a headache before the afternoon was over. As the crucial moment drew near, she regretted she hadn't persisted and found a pair of fancier slippers to wear. Her emerald gown was waltz length, about six inches from the floor. Her dark green pumps didn't lend the right festive touch.

But it didn't matter. All eyes would be on the bride. Before the last-minute jitters could escalate to absolute panic, the swell of organ music boomed and Robyn took a deep breath before beginning the long, stately walk up the church aisle. The church looked beautiful. The altar was massed with red and white flowers. Why did everyone want a June wedding? Sean and Meg would probably be having a June wedding. No, don't think of Sean.

Her eyes flew to the front of the church where he stood, his wide shoulders a bulwark of solidity. *I love him so much! Don't think of that.*

The guests craned their necks to see the wedding party come down the aisle. She was right: they hardly glanced at her. It was Noreen they were all gazing at. Soon they'd be gazing at Meg Britten. She'd make a beautiful bride. Sean would be standing on the other side of the altar then, waiting for his bride to join him before the minister. *Oh, Lord, I'm going to cry.*

Look at the stained-glass windows. They almost look electric, they're so bright in the sun. Like Christmas-tree lights. Christmas—when Sean had proposed to Meg. *Don't look at the windows. Look at the guests.* Funny how Mrs. Pender's white coat looked all red and green from the stained glass. Like Joseph's coat of many colors in the Bible.

At last the long, solemn march was over. Sean turned and flashed her a brief, nervous smile when she took her place beside him. He looked pale. What thoughts were whirling through his mind as he stood there, rigid as a toy soldier? Was he thinking this was the only time they'd stand together in front of a minister? Did he feel as desolate as she did?

I can't go through with it, Sean thought. I can't marry Meg Britten. It isn't fair to any of us, not even to Meg. She deserves better. It isn't right to marry a woman you don't love. I'll talk to her, tell her—what? Sorry, my dear, but I find I don't want to marry you after all. I love Robyn Halton. I always did. How beautiful she looks in green, like a wood nymph. She'd look even better in white lace. I want to hold her in my arms. I can't marry Meg. I can't. Oh, Lord, how can I get out of it? It would be a lousy thing to do.

"The ring," Rob whispered, and nudged his elbow.

Sean jerked himself back to attention and handed Ed the ring. He watched with interest as Ed slid it onto Noreen's fingers. "With this ring, I thee wed."

Sean had missed the best part of the wedding. All the moving pledge of the couple's troth. Such a strange, archaic word. Troth. Betrothed. He was betrothed to Meg. It meant he had pledged his fidelity to her.

His gaze slid to Robyn. In profile she looked like a Victorian cameo, so still. Why was her jaw locked in that hard line? She was trying not to cry. She never used to cry, but when she turned toward him to take his arm for the march back down the aisle, tears pooled in her great gold eyes. No one else had eyes the color of Robyn's. There was no one else in the world remotely like her.

She was smiling through her tears, but she felt just the way he felt, as if her insides had been ripped out. When the endless trip down the aisle was over, Jill and her escort drove with them to the hotel, so they couldn't say anything that mattered. Jill chattered like a magpie, which was just as well. Sean couldn't think of a word to say, and apparently Rob was similarly afflicted. In fact, she didn't even look at him. She looked out the window, wearing the saddest face he'd ever seen.

When they reached the hotel, there were pictures to be taken. They had decided not to take them outside the church, because of the weather. Later Sean looked around and saw that Meg had arrived. Why couldn't he love her? She was the most beautiful woman at the wedding, the most beautiful woman in Brooktown. That brilliant blue dress didn't do her pale coloring justice.

"It was a beautiful wedding." Meg smiled and put her hand on his arm. She thought Sean would say something romantic at this poignant moment.

"I nearly botched it. I couldn't locate the ring at the last minute," he replied.

The noisy crowd thronged around the punch bowl, discussing the beauty of the bride. Jill surreptitiously snatched a glass of the punch and drank it quickly before anyone noticed. It tasted just like fruit juice.

Eventually the party made its way to the dining room. The meal seemed endless. Robyn had to sit beside Sean at the head table, but she was acutely aware of Meg sitting just below them, keeping a sharp eye on Sean. Robyn felt like a felon every time she spoke to him, and she knew Sean felt the same way.

During this last time they would be more or less alone together, they made trite compliments on the wedding feast, which remained largely uneaten on both their plates. Only the darting glances of their eyes spoke their true thoughts. There were numerous toasts to the bride and the couple. Sean, among others, gave a short speech.

At last it was time to cut the three-tiered wedding cake. It looked so beautiful it seemed a shame to do it. Then the party moved to the ballroom, where an orchestra played the wedding waltz, and Ed and Noreen started the dancing. Later the others joined in.

"What a perfect little wedding," Meg sighed, and took Sean's hand to draw him onto the floor. "Ours will be much bigger. I plan to wear white satin."

Sean knew this was obviously not the time or place to confront Meg with the awful truth. He feared he couldn't tell her at all. He'd just have to grit his teeth and go through with it. He put his arms around her and they began dancing.

"Will you mind very much if we don't have a June wedding, Sean?" Meg asked.

"We hadn't firmly decided on June. Why?"

"If *Pygmalion* wins the competition, I'd be pretty busy in June." She listened to hear any signs of anger. "I thought September would be a good time."

"A fall wedding's nice," he agreed.

"You don't mind putting it off a little?"

"I know your acting's important to you."

"Not more important than you!" she assured him. But she was practically telling him the acting came first.

"It'll give us time to fix up the house," Sean said with very little enthusiasm.

"Yes, it needs a lot of modernization," Meg replied, carefully choosing her words. "Those old bathrooms, for instance."

"I thought you liked the marble tub."

"As sculpture, not as a working tub. But you can leave all that up to me. I'll tell you exactly what I want."

"I have some ideas, too. We'll talk it over later," Sean said with so little interest that the subject fell to the ground.

"I hear Rob Halton's not coming back home after all," she said, and watched closely for his reaction.

His body stiffened. "So she tells me."

"I wonder why."

"No doubt she has her reasons."

"I think it's downright selfish of her not to help out when Ed needs her."

She had her angry reaction now. The name Robyn Halton was the only goad he needed. "Rob's not selfish. That isn't why she's going back."

"Did she tell you why, when she got you into that dark corner last night?"

"No. And she didn't *get* me into a dark corner."

"Are you telling me *you're* the one who suggested it?"

"We were talking, Meg. That's all. Don't go imagining Rob's chasing after me. She isn't."

Meg gave a little laugh. "Let's not argue about Robyn. We can find more interesting things to fight about."

"I don't see why we should fight at all. You look very pretty tonight, Meg."

If he cared, he'd fight. Sean didn't love her. She loved him, or was very much attracted to him at least, but she wouldn't settle for a man who didn't love her to the very edge of insanity. When the dance was over, they changed partners and the dancing continued.

At seven-thirty Noreen went upstairs to change into her traveling outfit. The couple's flight to the Bahamas left at nine. Everyone crowded around the raised platform, waiting for Noreen to throw her bouquet. She took careful aim and tossed it in Robyn's direction. It sailed right over her head. Jill, standing behind her, jumped up and caught it, giving everyone a good laugh.

Robyn worked her way through the crowd to go to the door with Ed and Noreen, to wish them bon voyage. A few others came as well: Noreen's parents, Mrs. Halton and Jill. Sean began working his way in the same direction, and Meg followed a little distance behind. The couple left in a hail of rice and confetti and a shower of good wishes.

Mrs. Halton and Mrs. Crawley exchanged moist eyed but satisfied smiles. "That went off pretty well," Mrs. Crawley said. "I'm glad we don't have to do this every year. Noreen's my last. You still have Robyn and Jill to see launched."

"Not for a while, I hope," Mrs. Halton replied, smiling at Robyn. "Oh, my goodness! It slipped my mind, Rob. Jeff Perkins called the house just after you left. He wants you to call him. He said something about his plane landing in Watertown tomorrow morning, and getting a lift to Syracuse with you. He asked you to call him."

"I wouldn't mind the company," Robyn said.

"He said he'd be in Watertown in the morning—eight o'clock I think it was. I told him you have Monday off, dear," her mother reminded her.

Leaving a day early seemed like a very good idea. There were too many memories in Brooktown. "One day doesn't make much difference," Robyn said.

"It's up to you." Her mother looked disappointed but didn't object.

Sean frowned, and before long he worked his way to Robyn's side. "I don't see why you have to jump at Jeff's word. Your mother would like your company for another day. She'll be lonesome with Ed gone."

Robyn turned a stiff face to Sean and answered in a low but angry voice, "This has nothing to do with you, Sean. Butt out."

"The hell I will!"

"Then you can argue with yourself," Robyn retaliated, and swept off into the hall.

Sean followed her and stopped her with a hand on the elbow. "You said it was all over between you and Jeff," he said. There was a hint of accusation in his tone.

"I said I don't love him."

"Then why are you changing your plans to accommodate him?" he demanded angrily.

Robyn wrenched her arm free and tossed him a hard look. "That's none of your business."

She expected to see anger and was caught off guard by the serious, intent expression in his eyes. His voice sounded hollow in the narrow passage. "Robyn, I have to know" was all he said, but he said it with such intensity that she was astonished.

"Why? It has nothing to do with you."

"Yes, it has, and you know it."

She was blinded by the shock of certain knowledge. Sean had some plan to extricate himself from his engagement to Meg. Her heart pounded, and when she spoke her voice was a whisper. "What do you mean?"

"I can't say anything yet."

"Sean!" Hope soared and echoed in her voice.

"Well, are you going with him?" Sean asked. A pulse beat in his temple. *Please God, make her say no,* he prayed.

"Unless you can give me a good reason why I shouldn't."

"I can't—not yet."

The agony of suspense was unbearable. He couldn't expect her to be patient at a time like this. Half-mad with hope and fear, she said, "If I'm leaving at seven in the morning, I have to pack tonight. I also have to phone Jeff. I can't stay here all night."

"Dammit, Robyn, you can't expect me to get this straightened out in two minutes."

"All you have to do is tell Meg, Sean. I plan to leave in about an hour."

A group of wedding guests came along the passage and their private talk was interrupted. Robyn was trembling, and she went to the washroom to try to calm down.

Her insides were shaking with anxiety. She hardly dared to hope that everything was going to be all right. Had she given Sean enough time? An hour was plenty long enough to clear up the details. It stretched before her, seeming an infinity. Sixty minutes, thirty-six hundred slow seconds. A lifetime.

She should have known Sean would find a way.
Sean always worked things out. Robyn couldn't return to the party; her nerves were too ragged with
worry. Meg must have some idea that her romance
with Sean wasn't working out. Maybe they'd had a
fight already. Sean seemed pretty sure he could get out
of his engagement. Meg had been suspicious last
night. She must have said something to Sean. His
quick temper had flared, causing a fight. Or maybe it
was the house and the delaying of the wedding that
had caused it.

When some other guests entered the washroom,
Robyn left. She didn't want to go back to the ballroom, so she went into the hotel bar and ordered a
glass of wine to steady her nerves. The place was
nearly empty. She sat alone in a corner booth, hardly
daring to hope her life was going to be rescued by
Sean. The minutes dragged by. Five minutes, three
hundred seconds. Ten minutes, six hundred seconds.
Only fifty minutes to wait. Her wineglass was empty
already. She'd have another glass to dull the sharp
edge of anxiety.

What if Meg refused to give him up? Couples didn't
break up over a little thing like the man talking to an
old girlfriend. They had arguments, but breaking off
an engagement needed a more serious reason. She
must trust Sean. He had something in mind, or he
wouldn't have given her that ray of hope. He couldn't
be so cruel as to have given her hope if he didn't have
a plan. Would the time never pass? When Robyn
looked at her watch again, twenty minutes had
elapsed. Only forty minutes to go.

Sean's heart hammered with hostility when he heard about Jeff's phone call. Hostility and anxious impatience. He thought the Jeff thing wasn't serious, but Robyn's pride would deny a serious interest till she had Jeff secured. He thought he had a while to disengage himself from Meg. They had never acted like an engaged couple. Her dramatics meant more to her than he did. He had hoped to end it discreetly, with a minimum of hard feelings. And now Robyn had suddenly laid this impossible time limit on him.

How did you break off with your fiancée in one hour? Especially when you were at a public party? It couldn't be done. But in one hour Robyn would phone Jeff and arrange to drive him back to Syracuse. Let her do it, then. If she thought she had a ring through his nose she was wrong. A man could only bend over so far. It must be Jeff she really loved. She wasn't willing to risk losing *him*. Oh no, for Jeff she was willing to change all her plans, but she gave Sean just one hour to change the course of his whole life. He went back to the party and danced with Mrs. Crawley and Mrs. Halton and Jill.

"Where's your sister?" he asked Jill.

"I haven't seen her for a while. But don't worry that I've done anything you won't like, Sean. I've butted out," Jill assured him.

"The woman's impossible," Sean said to relieve the unbearable tension.

Jill was curious, and when she left Sean, she went looking for Robyn. After five more minutes, she found her in the bar.

"What are you doing in here?" Jill demanded. "You should be at the party."

"I'm waiting," Robyn said.

"For the party to get over, you mean?"

Robyn gave her a curious look. "No, for my party to begin," she said. "Have you seen Sean and Meg?"

"They're at the dance. Why?" Jill asked curiously.

Robyn frowned. "Are they—dancing?" she asked. She thought Sean would talk to Meg privately.

"Yes, but not with each other. Sean danced with me and Mom and Noreen's mother. Meg's dancing with Noreen's cousins."

"Hasn't he spoken to Meg at all?" Robyn asked.

"Not lately."

"Did he say anything about me?" Robyn asked.

"He said you were impossible. What's going on, Rob? Are you two fighting again?"

Robyn picked up her purse. Fifty of the sixty minutes were over, and Sean hadn't even spoken to Meg or tried to. He was dancing, if you pleased, while Robyn ate her heart out, worrying. "No, we're not fighting," she said coolly.

Her feet were a little unsteady when she stood up. The two glasses of wine on top of the wedding toasts had made her tipsy. It was all that kept her from going insane. She needed something to blunt the edge of her disappointment in Sean.

"Where are you going?" Jill demanded.

"I'm going up to my room. I vant to be alone," Robyn said, imitating Greta Garbo. Then she gave a laugh that sounded a lot like a cry and hurried out. She met a waiter carrying a tray and took a half-full bottle of champagne and a glass with her.

Jill watched the elevator and saw that Robyn had gone up to the suite that would have been hers, had she stayed. Only she wasn't staying, and the living room wasn't even furnished. What did she plan to do up there? Maybe she was just going to lie down for a while. She was talking a little funny, and her step was uncertain.

Jill shrugged and returned to the ballroom. A few guests were starting to act silly. She didn't want to miss out on the fun if any of them got loaded.

Chapter Eight

Since she'd been helping out at the hotel Robyn had carried a master key to all the rooms in her purse. She used the key to let herself into the unfinished suite. She'd thought when she decided to come up here that she was going to cry, and she wanted to do it in private. But once she was alone in the cool, silent room, the tears didn't come. Her eyes were hot and stinging, but there were no tears. She was too upset.

She just stood in the dark, looking around at the room. Moonlight reflecting from the stark white walls gave all the illumination she wanted. If she couldn't marry Sean, at least this suite should be her new home. In her mind she furnished it as she had planned, with the things from her Syracuse apartment—Wedgwood-blue drapes; the white-and-blue Oriental carpet that, though small, would cover most of the floor; the low, squashy, oatmeal-colored sofa that would go on the wall across from the window.

Should she paper the walls? Her modern paintings looked best against an unadorned surface. The smaller pieces, wooden tables and bookcase were stained very dark to contrast with the off-white of walls and floor. It would look lovely, but because of Sean Blake, she couldn't live here.

Sean was the only reason she'd left in the first place. It seemed he ruled her life, one way or the other. How dare he forbid her to come back, as he had done in this very room. "Why do you think?" he had asked, with that tormented grimace on his face. It was no consolation at all that Sean was hurting, too.

How dare he object to her "accommodating" Jeff Perkins? She might as well. No one was accommodating *her*, least of all Sean. And when all this futile fuming was finished, she went into the bedroom and sat forlornly on the end of the bed, wondering why he hadn't told Meg it was over between them.

He didn't care. That's all. He just didn't care that she'd spent the past hour sitting on thorns, waiting to hear whether she had a future to look forward to. If he loved her, he wouldn't have put her through that torment. But he *did* love her. She knew in her heart he loved her as much as she loved him. Meg had refused to give him up; that's what it was. Sean was honorable. He wouldn't renege if Meg dug in her heels. And why should she expect Meg to give him up? It was her own fault. She, Robyn Halton, had created this hellish situation.

Robyn saw the bottle of champagne glinting darkly in the moonlight and was surprised. She didn't remember bringing it up with her, but since it was here, a glass might subdue the ache in her heart.

It was a pervasive ache that spread out through her whole chest and stomach. Her head pounded. She pulled off the veil. The bottle of champagne was so heavy it wobbled when she poured the wine into the glass. But the wine tasted good. It still had some bubbles that broke against her nose when she drank. If she drank it quickly, maybe the pain would go away. She tilted the glass and drank half of it, then filled the glass and sat smiling in the darkness.

There, she felt better already. What did she care about Sean Blake? She didn't need him. She didn't need anyone. She'd be an island, standing alone in the stormy sea of life. She'd do exactly what she wanted to. If she wanted to come back to Brooktown, she'd come, and bring her blue drapes and blue-and-white carpet with her. Sean didn't own the color blue, just because he'd put it on his staircase. For her! *Surely* for her. Meg didn't even like it. She thought it looked dusty.

The tears that Robyn had been holding back for so long—ever since she came home—ever since she'd left—began trickling hotly down her cheek, and she wasn't even aware of them. But she knew she wasn't an island. She was a peninsula, and some part of her would always be attached to Sean.

Half an hour later Jill glanced at her watch and began to worry about Robyn. Maybe she should go up and check on her. She took the elevator up to the fourth floor. The door of the unoccupied suite was ajar, but the lights were off. Jill went in and flicked the switch. She looked around the empty living room, frowning.

From the other room she heard a sniffle, then a wispy voice called, "Turn off the lights. They're hurting my eyes."

Jill went to the doorway and peeped in. There sat Robyn on the end of the bed, holding a glass of champagne at a precarious angle. She wore a wobbly smile that set uneasily on her tear-stained face.

"Robyn, are you *drunk*?" she exclaimed.

"Nope, but I'm soon going to be," Robyn answered pertly.

"Why are you crying?"

"I'm not crying! Why should I cry? I'm happy," she sniffed.

"Your face is wet."

Robyn's face crumpled into tears. "I always cry at weddings," she said, and let the tears come coursing down her cheeks. "But I'm not sad. I'm very happy everybody is getting married. Everybody but me. Ed and Noreen, Meg and Sean . . ."

Jill advanced warily into the room and took the glass from Robyn's hand. She saw the nearly empty champagne bottle on the floor and took it, too. "Why don't you lie down and sleep it off, Rob? I'll tell Mom you have a headache. In fact, I think you'd better sleep here tonight. Boy, I see what you meant about wine going to your head. I wouldn't want you making a fool of yourself in front of all the guests."

Robyn folded her hands prissily in her lap. "I never make a fool of myself," she said, and burst out laughing, or maybe she was crying. Jill wasn't sure. It was a peculiarly desperate sound.

"Did something happen, Rob?" she asked.

"No, nothing happened. The hour's passed, and nothing happened. Nothing at all. Tomorrow I'll be accommodating Jeff Perkins. Nothing will happen there, either, but don't you dare tell Sean."

Jill tried to make some sense of this rubbish, but decided it was the wine talking. She got Robyn to lie down and went quietly out, turning off the lights on her way. She locked the door but got the key from the desk so she could come up again later and check on Robyn.

She went to the ballroom and sat pondering what could have happened. She saw Sean scanning the floor from the other side of the room. She lifted her chin and gave him a mutinous glare for having hurt Rob.

Sean saw that glare and wondered. Jill knew something. He strode purposefully across the floor. "Where's Rob?" he demanded."

"Leave her alone. You've done enough harm."

"Where is she?" he repeated, his voice becoming louder. "Has she gone home?"

"Yes," Jill said loud and clear.

Sean turned on his heel and stalked out of the hotel. Jill followed to see where he went. He went to the parking lot and saw Robyn's Reliant. Muttering a curse, he strode back. Jill was just hurrying down the corridor away from him. She heard his shout, but kept on going. Sean's long legs moved swiftly to cover the distance between them. He caught her a few yards from the elevator door. She turned toward the lobby so he wouldn't know Robyn was upstairs.

Sean put a hand on Jill's elbow and dragged her to a corner of the lobby. She sat on one of the sofas before he could push her onto it and scowled at him when he sat beside her.

"All right, brat, where is she?" he growled.

Jill's amber eyes flashed dangerously. "If you want to know, I think you're horrible," she said in a scornful tone.

"The situation is horrible. You had a good part in creating it," he reminded her.

Jill tilted her chin and looked away. A strong finger came out and pulled her head back, forcing her to look at him. Sean had a strange feeling of déjà vu when he looked into the speaking eyes that were so very much like Robyn's.

"I know it!" she said curtly. "I *tried* to make things right, but I couldn't do it all by myself. If adults can't straighten out their lives, what do you expect *me* to do?"

"Just tell me where she is."

"I can't."

Sean gritted his teeth in impatience and clenched his hands into fists. "How did I ever get mixed up with such impossible women! If you don't tell me where she is, Jill, I'm going to—"

Jill lifted a brow and gave him a derisive look. "You really should watch that temper, Sean. It's what Robyn dislikes most about you."

"She's in this hotel somewhere," he said, and jumped up.

Jill watched as he stormed into the manager's office. It was her chance to warn Robyn. She didn't know exactly what they could do, but at least she could let Rob know he was looking for her. She ran to the elevator and pushed the button. Her skirt was just disappearing behind the door when Sean came out of the office. He knew then where Robyn was hiding. He didn't wait for the elevator, but ran up the three flights of stairs.

When the elevator door opened, he reached out and took the key from Jill's hand. "Thanks, Jill. You can run along now."

Jill scanned her mind for some way to stop him and said with an air of important menace, "She'll never forgive you if you go in there now. *Never!*"

"Why not?"

"She'd die if you saw her intoxicated, and with—"

Jill suspected a threat of Robyn's undying wrath would be a deterrent. She didn't expect Sean to turn into a statue before her very eyes. He looked as if he were made of stone, except for the blue fire raging in his eyes. His voice, when he spoke, sounded like the voice of doom.

"Who's she with?" he demanded.

It took Jill a moment to figure out what he meant. She gasped and lifted her hand to slap him. His hand came out and grabbed her arm. "I said who is she with!" His voice lashed the air like a whip.

Undaunted, Jill lifted her foot and stomped the high heel of her shoe on his toe as hard as she could. The shock and pain made Sean release his grasp.

"I don't know what she ever saw in you! She's not with anyone. She drank too much wine because *you* hurt her. She wouldn't want you to see her with tears in her eyes. She's alone, crying her eyes out because *you* broke her heart. Now I hope you're satisfied," Jill said, and broke into tears herself.

Sean had graphic proof of the harm he'd done. Jill's tear-filled eyes were enough like Robyn's to make him feel like a monster.

"I'm sorry, Jill," he said gently.

"A lot of good that does!" She pushed the elevator button and went downstairs.

Sean already felt like a sinner when he went to the suite at the end of the hall. How was he supposed to get out of an engagement in the middle of a wedding party? A one-hour period was totally unreasonable. He meant to talk it over with Meg after the party. It was a conversation he looked forward to with dread, but marrying a woman he didn't love was worse. To think of Robyn marrying anyone else was impossible. He'd go mad.

Anger and guilt and uncertainty filled him with frustration as he quietly slid the key into the lock and opened the door. He was surprised to see the rooms were dark. Was Jill playing another stunt? He flipped on the light switch and immediately Robyn called from the other room, "Turn that light off, Jill!"

Her voice sounded muffled. Sean turned the light off and went to the connecting door. The carpet softened his footfalls as he approached. He could only distinguish outlines, but he knew the body on the bed must be Robyn's. "Go away, Jill," she said without even looking up.

As his eyes adjusted to the darkness, Sean saw that she lay facedown with her head turned toward the wall. He knew proud Robyn wouldn't want him there to see her tears. She was sniffling softly into the pillow.

"Is Sean still down there, dancing?" she asked in a hard voice.

His first surge of joy that she was thinking of him, that he was the first person she asked about, was tempered by her tears. Sean felt a deep stab of regret that he had made her so unhappy. "No, I'm here," he answered.

The dark form on the bed was galvanized into motion. Robyn popped up like a jack-in-the-box. "What are you doing here?" she demanded once again. The words had an awful air of repetition. She lifted her hand to straighten her hair and was grateful for the concealing darkness. It was unthinkable that Sean should see she was crying. Her jaw stiffened to prevent sniffling.

"Robyn—darling, I'm sorry," Sean said, and went to the bed. He sat tentatively on the edge of it and reached for her fingers.

Robyn pulled her hand away as though he were on fire. He hadn't managed to free himself from Meg. He pitied her and had come to commiserate! She was grateful for the swell of indignation that rose up to give her strength.

"Sorry for what?" she asked in a tense voice.

She felt his fingers on her cheeks, gently wiping away the tears, and twitched her head aside. His touch was like electricity. It sent a wave of longing through her.

"For this," Sean said simply. There was no arrogance in his words. He was simply stating a fact.

Angry and shamed that he knew she was crying, Robyn said, "Don't feel sorry for me. I'm delighted with the way things turned out."

"People don't weep from delight."

Robyn gave a mental wince of embarrassment. "I was thinking of other things. You seem to forget my father died not too long ago. Now Ed's married, the family is all breaking up." It made an excuse for the hiccup of regret she couldn't quite contain.

Sean's arms went around her, pulling her head against his chest. "I know. It's been a tough time for you." His fingers were in her hair, mauling it with familiar comfort.

Robyn's mind was fogged with the wine's hazy glow. When Sean held her in his arms as she had wanted for so long it was easy to forget he was no longer hers. And he wanted her, too. His touch wasn't the disinterested touch of a man comforting a stranger in distress. She knew all Sean's moods; they were etched deeply in her memory. There was longing desire in the caress of his fingers now. They clung warmly, intimately to the nape of her neck.

She felt a weakening wash of love course through her veins. How many lonely nights had she dreamed she was here, where she belonged? She stirred in his arms and emitted a long sigh. It set off a rush of dangerous desire in Sean, and his fingers fell still.

He shouldn't be here alone with Robyn like this. He'd just stay till she settled down. He wouldn't kiss her. He *wouldn't*. But his lips tingled with the remembered thrill of past kisses. It wasn't like that, kissing Meg. His whole being wasn't drawn into the experience, mind and soul as well as heart and body.

Robyn rubbed her cheek against his chest and murmured, "Don't stop. That felt so good."

Her voice, softened to a plea, sent a quiver through him. Sean swallowed carefully and began moving his fingers very slowly and very lightly. How much more of this divine torture could he take? Robyn's body was softly yielding in his arms. Her crooning voice was an encouragement to intimacy. He felt instinctively she wouldn't stop him if he tried to kiss her and was surprised that Robyn was behaving like this.

She lifted her head. He saw by the moonlight the tears drying on her cheeks but her lashes were still matted with tears, and her lips drooped. The lingering aroma of wine assailed him. Jill had mentioned she'd drunk too much wine. In the chaos of trying to find her, he'd forgotten. That's why she was letting him hold her. But if she continued encouraging him, he wouldn't be able to resist her.

He could hardly hold himself in check when he looked at her sad face bathed in moonlight. How had he ever thought he could live without her? Why hadn't he gone to Syracuse and *made* her marry him when Jill first told him about Jeff Perkins? Most of all, why had he asked Meg to marry him? Two wrongs didn't make a right. It would be a sin to marry anyone but Robyn.

"It's going to be all right, darling," he said. His voice was ragged and uneven from the exertion of self-denial.

Robyn's lips formed a sulky pout. "The hour passed. You didn't tell Meg." A fresh tear oozed down her cheek. "I waited and waited, but you didn't come. If you loved me..."

"I love you!" His voice was harsh. "I've *always* loved you. I love you too much."

Robyn closed her eyes and released a shuddering sigh. *He loves me! He does!* She felt as if a heavy stone had fallen from her heart. She felt light-headed, giddy with relief and joy. "Then kiss me!" She smiled and lifted her face.

Sean gulped. "I—I haven't straightened things out with Meg yet, Rob."

"You'd better do it very soon, Sean Blake. Because you love me and I love you, and I'm going to kiss you, whether you're engaged to somebody else or not."

She placed her lips on his and threw her arms around his neck in a heady swirl of joy. Sean pulled back, but she pursued him, pulling him more closely against her. A glow of exultation suffused her when he stopped struggling. First the resistance went out of him, and he let her hold him. Then she pressed against him, and he put his arms around her.

Sean couldn't hold back any longer. The fury of three long years' frustration overcame him, and he crushed Robyn in his arms while his lips bruised hers in a torturing kiss that still wasn't enough. Once his defenses were breached, the pent-up flow of love and passion came washing over him like a tide. It had been too long. He had been too afraid of losing her and he loved her too much to stop now.

His hands stroked her back and shoulders roughly in a fever of impatience to claim her for his own. He had to confirm this was really happening, and that it wasn't another dream. If it was a dream, he never wanted to awaken. He wanted to go on holding Rob and kissing her till he died of sheer ecstasy.

A hot tumult of passion built inside as he embraced her, and she returned every frenzied stroke.

The thrust of her full breasts against his chest tantalized him with their feminine softness.

His parted lips tasted champagne, reminding him of her condition. But it didn't matter. Nothing mattered but that they were together at last. His tongue stroked her lips, savoring them, and then she opened her mouth and drew him into its silken intimacy, hungrily, greedily, intoxicating him with her passion. Sean felt he was drowning in bliss, drugged with love, unable to make her stop. Oh, God, if she didn't stop soon . . . But he wanted the kiss to go on forever.

He made one final effort to release her. He put his hands on her shoulders and gently pushed her away. Robyn gazed at him from eyes glazed with tears and wine and passion. "I love you so much, Sean," she said. Her voice was breathless and quaking, like a little girl's voice, but her body was all soft, alluring femininity.

An agonized groan sounded in his throat, and he buried his face in the crook of her neck. A throbbing need grew in him. "You've got to help me, Rob," he begged, his voice hoarse.

"You know I'd do anything for you," she breathed in his ear. Her lips seized one lobe and her tongue flicked moistly over it. The smooth edge of her teeth grazed his flesh. He felt her vital breaths reverberating softly, irresistibly in his head.

They shattered the last of his control, and the words of love came pouring out. "You don't know how I've longed to hear you say that again, darling. I think I must have been mad when I heard you were going to marry Jeff. Mad, or a damned fool not to stop you."

Robyn gave an ecstatic gurgle and rubbed her forehead against his, while her fingers twined possessively in his luxuriously soft hair. Her eyes glittered with enchantment in her pale face. She turned her body fully against his and pushed him down on the bed, hovering above him.

Her silky hair played against his cheek. By the moon's pale light he saw her face glowing with love. She looked abandoned. She'd let him make love to her now. She expected it, but was it the effect of the wine?

They had never done it before and this was hardly the time to start. "I think we'd better—" Sean tried to raise himself from the bed, but she playfully pushed him down.

"I want you, Sean. I've wanted you for so long."

"And I want you, Robyn, but I think we really should go—now."

Her answer was a teasing invitation. "I think we should stay," she said, and lowered herself to kiss him.

This new aggressiveness stunned Sean. Robyn had never thrown herself at him in this way before. He had been the aggressor, but he soon discovered he liked this independent streak. She pressed her body against his, while her hands and lips began a frenzied exploration of his body. After a scuffle at his shirt front, he felt her fingers curling in the crisp hair of his chest, drawing tickling circles with her long fingernails.

"Why are we wearing so many clothes? I want to feel you," she whispered in a dreamy voice.

Sean had given up the struggle to keep his shirt closed. His hands rested on the swell of her hips, which lay close against his own. He could feel her soft warmth all along his body, urging him on to madness. And if he didn't get out of here now, he'd do something they'd both regret.

With the last of his control, he tightened his hold on her hips and lifted her bodily aside. Robyn sat a moment, blinking in surprise at the abrupt movement.

"I'm going now," Sean said firmly, and pushed himself to the edge of the bed.

She blinked in surprise. "Where?"

"Downstairs. I suggest you tidy your hair and come down, too. People will be wondering what's happened to us." He stood up reluctantly and began buttoning his shirt.

Robyn watched, with surprise turning to disappointment. The heady intoxication of champagne was beginning to ebb. "You mean Meg'll be wondering," she interpreted, in a voice that tweaked his temper.

"I imagine she will," he said with a worried frown. "She's still my fiancée, after all."

But he said he loved *Robyn*. She was losing him again. No, she had never recaptured him. He belonged to Meg, and Sean was too honorable to be unfaithful to his fiancée. What must he think of her, throwing herself at him? He despised her. And no wonder; she even despised herself. What madness had come over her? She felt cheap and degraded by the experience. She couldn't let him leave, not like this. She had to do something to detain him.

In a fuzzy, wine-tinged flurry of desperation she said, "What must you think of me, Sean? I'm afraid I had too much champagne tonight. That's why I—"

He cut her off abruptly. "I hope it wasn't just the wine." His questioning look demanded reassurance.

"Maybe your being here had a little something to do with it." She gave a deprecatory smile that warmed him.

"Don't scare me like that! I have to go now, Rob. You come down as soon as you've tidied yourself up." He went to the door, but before he left he flicked on the light switch.

Robyn knew she was all disheveled and didn't want him to see her like that. "Please turn that off!" she said.

"I want to be sure it was really you on that bed. You seemed—different. That's not a complaint, just an observation."

Robyn was uneasy with his dark eyes gazing at her. "Maybe we should have a good look at ourselves. We're supposed to be civilized human beings. You have a fiancée downstairs, and we were acting like animals."

Robyn couldn't see herself, but she saw Sean's hair all mussed from her fingers. His face was flushed from the aftermath of their embraces. His shirt and tie were askew. She knew she must look even worse. She could see her gown was wrinkled and pulled aside.

Sean examined her closely. Ninety-nine percent of him wanted to go back to that bed and make violent love to Rob. The abandoned tousle of her hair was an invitation. Her lips were swollen from his kisses, and she sat with her legs curled enticingly under her. "We have animal urges. That's the way God made us." And his animal urges were still very active.

"What if..." Robyn swallowed and forced the question out. "What if Meg doesn't agree to break the engagement?"

Sean just closed his eyes and shook his head. It was unthinkable. "Meg's reasonable," he said, but Robyn noticed he was frowning.

They both knew Meg was also used to getting what she wanted, and she was very satisfied with her prospective bridegroom. Robyn looked so desolate that he went to the bed and patted her shoulder.

She lifted her head. Her smile was filled with fear and sadness. "I'm glad we had tonight anyway, Sean, even if we shouldn't have."

Caught up in their emotions, neither Robyn nor Sean had heard the outer door open. They didn't know Meg was there till she appeared at the open doorway. Her pretty face was pink with anger, and her blue eyes blazed. So this was how Sean behaved when he really loved someone! She'd never seen that tender glow in his eyes when he was with her. And Robyn Halton! She was shameless. What did she mean by "I'm glad we had tonight?"

"Am I interrupting something?" Meg asked, and stepped into the room.

Chapter Nine

Robyn and Sean exchanged a guilty look as Meg directed an accusing stare from one to the other.

"We were just—" Sean began, only to be interrupted by Robyn.

"Meg, this isn't what you—"

Meg walked to Sean and lifted her hands to straighten his tie. "You must be more careful, darling," she said with a strained smile. "The woods are full of predatory females. I think I know whose idea this was. The woman's desperate." She turned to give Robyn a dismissive look.

Robyn withered under that sneering insult. She looked expectantly at Sean, waiting for him to defend her, but Meg continued talking.

"Better luck next time, Robyn. This one's taken," she said, and linked her arm through Sean's to drag him away.

Sean hesitated a moment, but he wasn't sure what Meg might say, and he didn't want Robyn to hear in case it was too rough. Behind Meg's back he shrugged his shoulders, then left. He just walked out the door without even saying goodbye. Robyn stared after them, unable to believe that Sean hadn't said anything. It was the perfect opportunity to have it out with Meg. What had stopped him?

Hadn't he meant any of those things he'd said? When it came right down to it, would he have the guts to break off with Meg? Had he lost his head in the heat of passion? She moaned in chagrin. That was all she needed. The perfectly horrendous ending to a perfectly vile day. She might as well have tried to seduce Sean on a street corner. Meg couldn't be expected to keep this tidbit to herself. Robyn's shame and humiliation were complete.

The only easing of the darkness was that tomorrow she could leave Brooktown. In a few years, she might gather up her courage to come back. It didn't occur to her yet to wonder how Meg had found her and Sean.

It occurred to Sean a little sooner. The name Jill Halton was in his mind.

"How did you find us, Meg?" he asked. They were in the elevator, returning below.

"It was easy. I saw you talking to Jill, then disappearing upstairs. When Jill came down on the elevator, I asked her where you went. Of course she said she had no idea, but I kept an eye on her and followed her up later. When she opened the door, I pushed my way in. Jill looked as guilty as sin and disappeared. Just as well. There are some things a child shouldn't be exposed to," she added with an accusing look.

The elevator opened into the lobby, and they got out. "Let's get away from here," Meg suggested. "We have to talk in private." It sounded like a good idea to Sean.

They went to Meg's house, but she didn't invite him in. Their discussion took place in his car in front of her house. Her first bout of anger had passed. She had already confronted the idea that Sean didn't love her, and that made it easier.

"This isn't working out, is it, Sean?" she said. "When I agreed to marry you, I thought you were all over her."

Sean took her hand and squeezed it. "I thought so, too, Meg. I really had no idea this would happen. Rob wasn't herself tonight—too much celebrating. I've tried to fight it . . ."

"Fighting! That's how I knew you didn't really love me. You wouldn't fight with me—until I made the mistake of casting a slur on Robyn Halton."

"Meg, there are dozens of guys in this town who would give their eyeteeth for you."

"You just don't happen to be one of them, huh?"

"You're a beautiful, lovely woman."

"Thanks," she said resignedly. "I'm also spoiled. It happens when you're the only child of wealthy parents. I was afraid you'd go right on spoiling me as they'd done. You never showed much backbone with me. I didn't want that, you know. Would you not have tried to change me?"

"Probably not."

"Because you don't love me enough to bother. And I don't think I love you enough to let you succeed. Oh, well, Liza Doolittle didn't get her Henry Higgins, either. I'll just have to find myself a Freddie.''

Sean sighed in frustration. "I'm really very fond of you, Meg. But it wouldn't be fair of me to—to take you from some guy who'd love you more. You deserve the best.''

"You, too, Sean. But I think what you really want is Robyn Halton," she added snidely. "Why don't you go and tell her? She didn't expect you to leave with me.''

A smile of pleasure curved his lips. "She'll scratch my eyes out!''

Meg felt a twinge of regret. She envied Robyn the coming argument. "I doubt if she'll escape unscathed. Give her a thump for me.''

"I'll do that.'' Sean tried manfully to conceal his joy but failed quite miserably. He gazed at Meg a moment. "Would it sound too corny if I said I've enjoyed knowing you, Meg? I have, you know.''

"Same here. But don't talk as if we'll never see each other again. I don't intend to run away to Syracuse like some jilted ladies.''

"Good. Brooktown needs you. I'll be at your play to see you on opening night.''

Meg noticed he didn't even know the name of the play. "It's *Pygmalion*, Sean, based on the old Roman legend of a sculptor who carved a statue of a beautiful woman and fell in love with it. Aphrodite brought her to life for him. Galatea was her name.'' She felt a sense of loss. Sean could have brought her better qualities to life, if he'd loved her enough.

Meanwhile she'd gained some insights for the play. Her face assumed an artful pose of resigned sorrow.

Yes, this is how Liza must have felt when Henry Higgins forsook her. "Goodbye, Sean," she said, and gave him a parting kiss on the cheek.

"Goodbye, dear Meg."

"What you are to do without me I cannot imagine," she told Sean, and swept out of the car.

He gave a confused look, turned the key and drove quickly back to the hotel. His heart soared with joyful relief. He was free! Meg had been terrific—no scene, no tears. It was almost as if she was glad to get rid of him, which was a chastening thought. But his real interest was in the immediate future. Now he could take Robyn up on her persistent offer. He hoped she was still in the room where he'd left her, in bed. Impatience goaded him on to a reckless speed, but he made the trip without accident or police intervention.

He ran into the hotel lobby and pushed the elevator button seven times in his eagerness. When he got to the door of Robyn's suite, he rapped hard, calling out her name. Was she just not answering, or had she left? Finally he went down to the office and learned that Miss Halton had turned in the key and left. He went to the ballroom, but a quick search showed him Robyn wasn't there.

Jill was slinking guiltily in the shadows, trying not to be seen. Sean paced over to her. "Where is she?" he demanded.

Jill shrugged her shoulders. "I haven't seen her for ages," she said, carefully crossing her fingers behind her back.

She wasn't taking any more chances by interfering in other people's lives. Rob had nearly thrown a fit when she came downstairs, asking how Meg knew she was upstairs with Sean. Was it her fault if Meg followed her? She'd tried to keep her out of the room. Meg was stronger than she looked.

Sean didn't know Jill's habits as well as her sister did. He didn't recognize the telltale biting of her lip as a dead giveaway. He whirled away to see if Rob's car was gone from the parking lot. When he learned it was, he drove over to her house. There were no lights burning, but more conclusively, the light coating of newly fallen snow in the driveway was undisturbed. She hadn't been home since the early evening snowfall. Where could she be?

When Robyn left the hotel, she just wanted to be alone to lick her wounds. She wanted to go where no one could find her for an hour or so. Her head had stopped reeling, and she felt it was safe to drive. She drove to a little diner on the edge of town where she used to go with Sean, and hunkered down in a back booth with a cup of coffee.

With sobriety came the realization that she'd made a hideous scene. She'd thrown herself shamelessly at Sean and been rejected. That's what it came down to in the end. He hadn't explained things to Meg when he had the perfect opportunity. Meg knew everything, and in her temper she wouldn't keep it to herself. Robyn was disgraced and wished she could drive to Syracuse that very night. Her apartment there seemed like an oasis in the desert of her life. She had gotten over Sean there before, and at least she'd be away from the prying eyes of her friends and the commiserating expression of her mother. She really couldn't face all that.

After one cup of coffee, she remembered she hadn't returned Jeff's call. The drive to Syracuse with him was also unthinkable. She'd have to make polite conversation all the way and pretend she wasn't hurting inside. She called him at his home in Watertown and said she was sorry she wouldn't be returning to Syracuse tomorrow.

"When are you going?" he asked.

It was a perfectly logical question, but the answer stuck in her throat. Monday? She couldn't face a whole day at home, trying to act as though nothing had happened. "Tonight," she heard herself say. The answer came from her subconscious. It was what she wanted to do. Why not do it? The wedding was over. Her mother thought she'd be leaving tomorrow morning with Jeff, anyway. One night didn't make any difference. Her family thought she was romantically involved with Jeff. It would seem reasonable that she changed her plans to "accommodate" him, as Sean so deftly put it.

Once the decision was made, Robyn was impatient to get on with her departure. She drove home just minutes after Sean left. A phone call to the hotel was the only preparation needed, other than packing. She explained to her mother that she'd spoken to Jeff and decided to leave tonight. The details were left vague, but her mother concluded exactly what Robyn hoped.

"This is beginning to sound serious between you and Jeff. You must bring him home to meet us soon," she said.

"Yes."

"Then I won't see you again before you leave. I wish you'd reconsider coming home to live, Rob. It would be so nice to have you back in town, helping out at the hotel. Do think about it.''

The lump in Robyn's throat felt as big as a grapefruit. ''I will, Mom.'' I won't be able to think of anything else. ''Bye. I'll call real soon. I don't want to keep you from the party any longer. Say goodbye to Jill for me.''

''I will. Well, drive carefully, dear.''

''Don't worry.''

Robyn hung up and gave a long, weary sigh. She hated dissembling with her mother, but didn't want to worry her with the true story. She hoped Sean could convince Meg to keep quiet. Her leaving tonight might assuage Meg's anger. Meg couldn't think she was trying to steal Sean away if she wasn't even in town. Leaving was definitely the right thing to do, but her heart felt like a lead boulder at the thought of leaving all she loved and going back to Syracuse.

Would she ever be coming back to stay? At the moment it didn't look like it. As bad as this visit had been, any future one would be worse. Three years hadn't cured her of loving Sean. She doubted three centuries would do it. Her only small consolation was that he'd said he loved her. And in his way he did. But it seemed he was going to honor his commitment to Meg. Robyn really couldn't fault him for that.

Robyn was beyond tears. Her eyes were hot and dry when she took off her bridesmaid gown and hung it up. Slacks and a warm sweater were what she wanted for the trip. She quickly stuffed her clothing into her suitcase. She carried the big bag downstairs and carefully turned off all the lights before she left. The night air was still and cold. A bluish-yellow halo sur-

rounded the streetlights. The snow crunched under-
foot when she went to put her case into the trunk.

She was glad the snow made driving a little difficult. It demanded her attention and distracted her
from brooding about personal problems. At Watertown she thought of Jeff and felt bad about refusing
to drive him to Syracuse. But really she didn't want to
start seeing him again. It would be a long time before
she wanted to go out with anyone.

Just beyond Watertown a light sprinkling of snow
began to fall. It swirled like a lace curtain against the
windshield and slowed her speed. As she drove down
toward Oneida Lake, the snow became heavier. She
considered stopping overnight at a motel, but she was
so close to Syracuse that she forged on. The trip that
should have taken less than three hours took nearly
five. She was exhausted by the time she pulled into the
garage at her apartment building, and she uttered a
silent prayer that she'd made it home safely.

Home. This was her home now. She must forget
that other home. Yet when she switched on the light
in her little living room, every object reminded her of
Sean. The blue curtains were the same shade as the
carpet on his curving staircase, in the house where Jill
said he kept her picture in his bedroom. But it wasn't
true. She thought of Jill and gave a rueful smile. Poor
kid. She'd been pretty hard on Jill before she left.
She'd phone her soon and set things right. Jill was
only trying to help.

Robyn set the suitcase down and happened to notice the blue-and-white carpet. It would have looked
good in the hotel suite Ed had kept open for her.
"You're not coming back here! . . . I don't want you

here!'' That had been Sean's initial reaction. She should have listened. You couldn't recapture the past. It was too illusory, like a rainbow.

And she was too tired to go chasing rainbows tonight. She was grateful for the fatigue that dulled her senses. She left the case where she had dropped it at the arch of the living room and went into her bedroom. As she lay alone in bed, she could still hear the echo of humming tires in her ears. She imagined the snowflakes swirling hypnotically against the windshield. Always it seemed she was about to penetrate the curtain of gusting snow, but there was always another layer of it, waiting to obscure her vision.

She was glad she'd come back tonight. By tomorrow the roads might be impassable. There was no arguing with nature on a rampage. It swept everything before it, like a fierce passion. Now why did that make her think of Sean? Everything made her think of Sean. And why couldn't she sleep? She was dead tired. Her very bones ached from weariness, but sleep refused to come.

At that moment, with the arduous trip over, when she was safely lying in bed, her control broke. Sorrow swept over her in a deluge. She'd lost him forever. Tears scalded her eyes and trickled unchecked down her temples to wet her hair. His words echoed in her ears. ''Robyn—darling, I'm sorry.'' Oh, but not as sorry as she was! He'd forget her when he married Meg. Meg, with that scathing look over her shoulder as she straightened Sean's tie with a proprietary air, as though she was already his wife. And Sean hadn't uttered a word in Robyn's defense.

What had gotten into her to throw herself at him so shamelessly? It was panic, desperation—and champagne. It was one last futile effort to win him. And instead she had made a flaming fool of herself. She'd not only lost his heart, she'd lost her self-respect. Syracuse wasn't far enough away. She wished she could fly to some remote island and jump into a volcano.

When Sean didn't find Robyn at home, he returned to the hotel and learned that she wasn't there, either. Her car wasn't there. He didn't want to worry her mother by telling her Robyn was missing. Maybe she'd parked her car along the street and was hiding in some unoccupied room of the hotel. He got Jill's help to check out the register and get the keys to the unoccupied rooms. Jill refused, till he confided that Meg had set him free. Half an hour later, he knew Robyn wasn't in the hotel.

"She can't have just disappeared," Jill said, becoming worried. "I've got to tell Mom. She might be in an accident, Sean. It's snowing quite hard now."

A look of terror settled on Sean's face. "Oh, Lord, I never thought of that!" He pushed down the awful images that cropped so readily into his imagination.

Sean went with Jill to accost Mrs. Halton. "I know she's gone, dear," Mrs. Halton said calmly. "Rob called me from home. She decided to go back to Syracuse tonight. It seems Jeff Perkins was in some great rush, and she agreed to take him. I think we're going to be seeing a lot of that young man in the future."

"Jeff!" The word was out before Sean got control of himself. It was an unbelieving howl of protest.

"Well, really, Sean," Mrs. Halton sniffed, "I don't see that it has anything to do with you who Robyn goes out with."

Sean left and Jill followed him, curious to learn what he meant to do. Her hopes for a reconciliation had never quite died, and when Sean told her Meg had released him, she felt the thing was as good as settled. She danced along at Sean's elbow giving unwanted advice.

"What you have to do is go after them, Sean," she suggested. "Can I go with you, please? I'll be a big help. I know exactly where Rob's apartment is in Syracuse. You'd have trouble finding it."

"I'm not going after her," he growled. "She knew how I felt. She never had any intention of getting back with me. She just did it for spite."

"Robyn's not like that!" Jill defended hotly.

"She's exactly like that. She always went out with some guy she knew I hated when we had a fight. She knows my feelings about Jeff Perkins."

"You don't even *know* him," Jill pointed out.

"I don't have to know him. What kind of a jerk would ask a woman to drive him all the way to Syracuse in the middle of a snowstorm, and on the very night of her brother's wedding?"

Jill frowned. "Gee, that *is* funny," she said suspiciously.

"And what kind of a woman would agree to do it? A woman in love—that's what kind. She's loved Jeff all along. She only let on she was coming back to Brooktown to scare him into proposing."

"I don't think she loves him at all," Jill objected. "She said she'd only been out with him half a dozen times. And she *did* intend to come home to stay, till she heard about you being engaged to Meg."

"I don't want to hear any more of your tall tales," Sean said, and strode angrily into the bar.

The same instinct that had led Robyn to the isolated corner booth at the diner led Sean to the darkest corner of the bar. He didn't order a drink, but sat with his head propped on one hand, thinking. Common sense told him he was right. Rob had run away when he wouldn't hop to her tune three years ago. This time she'd run away on Jeff. But Jeff was wiser than he was; he'd agreed to whatever impossible demand Rob had made.

But if that was what had happened, why had she come on to him in the hotel? She already knew Jeff had called. Her mother had told her earlier, when Ed and Noreen were leaving, and Rob hadn't been in any hurry to call him back. No, what she'd done was get herself tipsy with champagne upstairs, alone.

It was the champagne that had caused her to throw herself at him. He knew that wasn't typical of Rob. But even drunk, she wouldn't have done it if she didn't love him. She *did* love him. He felt it in his bones and in his veins. It was only his damned Irish temper that kept them apart.

It was time to take command of his temper. He'd go after her, because if he didn't he'd spend the rest of his life wondering what had really happened here tonight. He'd spend a lifetime of regret if a word from him might have won her back. Instinct told him the word would be most effective if delivered in person.

He stood up resolutely and left the bar. He got his coat and went out to his car. The snow was flying thick and fast by that time. It would take him aeons to reach Syracuse, but Rob and Jeff couldn't be making very good time, either. In any case he'd certainly be there by morning, unless the highways were completely closed down.

Chapter Ten

The trouble with having come back to Syracuse early was that Robyn found herself faced with Sunday and Monday before she could go back to work. She had forty-eight long hours with nothing to do but regret her folly. The snow was a foot deep outside. It was a good day to stay home, and staying home gave her the added advantage of not having to get dressed. Robyn pulled her wool plaid housecoat around her and went to the bathroom. She felt sorry for the pitiful creature she saw in the mirror.

In her state of fatigue and distraction the night before, she hadn't even taken off her makeup. Black smudges under her eyes testified to that long bout of tears. Her hair hung like limp rope around her face, and her eyes looked strangely dead. A shower was definitely called for.

She let the warm water pelt her face, relishing the counterirritant. Then she adjusted the spray to hard for her back. The water needles pricking her shoulders felt as welcome as a new day. The woman in the mirror was beginning to look half-human after the shower. A cup of coffee might get her eyes completely open and maybe even put a touch of color in her cheeks.

While Robyn waited for the coffee to perk, she sat down and tried to take command of her life. She had all sorts of things to do, but when she tried to latch on to them, they had an obstinate way of scattering and leaving in their wake an image of Sean Blake. His dark blue eyes laughed at her from the door of the fridge. The hanging ivy by the window only partially concealed his silhouette, with the jet-black hair growing so neatly around his forehead.

Now why did the coffee canister have to be that deep blue, just the shade of his eyes? Was Sean having coffee now? He wouldn't be working on Sunday. He'd probably be coaching his hockey team, down at the river rink. She wondered if Jill would be there, looking for that boy called Harry. It had been fun, skating again. The muscles of her legs were still a little stiff. There were rinks in Syracuse, so there was no reason she couldn't go skating today, but she knew she wouldn't.

She'd make a list. That's what she'd do. The first priority was to take down the Christmas decorations and clean the apartment. There was nothing as sad as Christmas decorations after the festive season was over. Unless it was the bitter memories of romance after the love had died. Some evil genie prompted her to look at the calendar and she noticed it was the 31 December.

Tonight was New Year's Eve, that traditional night of special celebration. She hadn't made any plans, because she'd thought she'd be at home. Brooktown would always be her home. There was no point trying to force her mind to think she really lived here, in spite of the friends who were only a phone call away. Home was where the heart dwelt. The sound of hissing from the stove told her the coffee had boiled over while she sat staring mindlessly into space.

Robyn poured a cup. She thought the cream would probably be sour by now, but it smelled fine and didn't curdle. Amazing how they could preserve everything nowadays. Everything except... No, she was becoming morbid. Toast to go with the coffee? Yuck. Who could face food? The coffee tasted like wood. How could coffee taste so dry? She pushed it away and glanced at her watch. Good heavens, it was nine o'clock already. She really should get started on taking down the Christmas ornaments and cleaning the apartment.

When Sean finally reached Syracuse at eight o'clock the next morning, he found that the trouble with driving all night was that you arrived looking like a hobo. You had to go to a hotel to clean up before calling on the woman you love. He mentally castigated himself for having come without a change of clothes. The hotel provided a nice white terry bathrobe, however, and was helpful about laundering his clothes and brushing his suit while he showered.

The laundering and pressing took an hour, even with the hefty bribe, which left Sean in his room wearing only the terry-cloth coat. Maybe some breakfast would help to pass the time. He called room service and sat nervously on the end of the bed, trying to plan his strategy. He didn't even know where Rob lived. The phone book gave him the address, and another call downstairs provided him with a city road map.

He sipped the coffee while he studied it. When he had memorized his route, he lifted the lid from his breakfast, gazed with distaste at two shirred eggs, bacon and toast, and promptly replaced the lid. He couldn't eat a bite for the nervous knotting of his stomach. And what was keeping his clothes? It felt like hours since he'd sent them off. A glance at his watch told him it had been exactly twenty-five minutes.

Sean began pacing the room. Should he phone first? But if she refused to let him come... No, the thing to do was just go and present her with a fait accompli. And what if Jeff Perkins was there? His temple throbbed like a jungle drum. He had to remind himself there would be no unseemly display of temper. He was a reformed man.

After another endless thirty-five minutes, his clothes were brought to the door and Sean quickly put them on. Oblivious to how well they suited him, he thought he looked like an undertaker, decked out in the black suit so early in the morning. He was glad his overcoat covered most of it. The desk clerk was stunned to see Mr. Blake checking out so soon.

"Was there something wrong with your room, sir?" he asked.

"No, it was fine."

"But you just got here!"

"Yes, and now I have to leave," Sean replied vaguely. He didn't even notice that the clerk gave him a reduced rate.

Driving in a strange city with all but the major arteries snow-clogged was a hair-raising experience. One-way streets threw him off his course and cost him time. It was ten o'clock when he spotted Robyn's tall gray apartment block. The snow-removal team was just cleaning the visitors' lot, and he parked at one end while the plow drove along to the other.

A dozen problems swarmed through his mind as the hour of confrontation approached. Robyn might not even be up yet. When he entered the lobby, he found a bank of buzzers and names. Rob was on the seventh floor, in apartment 708. He'd have to buzz her before he could get into the elevators. He didn't want to let her know he was there until she opened her apartment door. He managed to get inside on the coattails of a resident and took the elevator up to the seventh floor.

Every nerve in his body was jumping by the time he found 708. He was unhappy to see a peephole in the door. He wanted to see her face the minute she first saw him. If she saw him, she might not open the door. On the other hand, she certainly wouldn't open it if he hid. It would look too suspicious.

Inside, Robyn was just putting the last of the outdated newspapers into a garbage bag to haul down to the incinerator shoot. She was hot and tired from the clean-up job, but the apartment was back to normal. Could she risk taking the bag down the hall in her housecoat? It was only a few yards away. She wouldn't bother getting dressed for that. She threw open the door and gave a stifled gasp.

Sean! She had finally flipped her lid. She'd been mentally seeing him all morning, and now he was really here, big as life, standing right in front of her. She slammed the door shut and stood trembling. Had she really seen him? Was it possible he was here, in Syracuse, in the flesh? She put her eye to the peephole and peered out. Sean stood looking blankly at the closed door with his mouth open. While she looked he raised his hand and knocked.

"Rob, can I come in for a minute?" he asked politely.

A smile of disbelief trembled on her lips and she reached for the doorknob. It had to be a dream. The real Sean would be battering down the door by now. She peered out again. He was biting his bottom lip in indecision, the way Jill did when she was making up some story. He looked tired and wan and uncertain, which was not at all the way she thought of Sean. But there was no doubt he was real.

Then Robyn glanced in the hall mirror and saw herself. Her hair was all mussed from vacuuming and cleaning. She didn't have on a drop of makeup, and she was still wearing her nightgown and housecoat. She couldn't let him see her like this.

Another knock sounded on the door, louder now. "I just want to talk to you," Sean called. His voice was louder, too, but still not at all demanding.

Her hands rose futilely to her hair. "Just a minute! Don't go away!" she called, and darted off for her purse. Just a quick flick of the hairbrush and a daub of lipstick. *My God,* she thought, *I look like a ghost.* From the living room, she heard the next knock, which was becoming noticeably peremptory now.

"Let me in, Rob. I've come all the way from Brooktown to see you." His voice held more than a tinge of polite impatience.

Her shaking fingers made a mess of the lipstick. She fumbled for a paper hankie to wipe it off the side of her face.

"Let me in or I'll break down the door!" The door rattled on its hinges from the force of his blows.

Oh yes, it was definitely Sean. The lips in her compact mirror stretched wide in a gleeful smile. A feeling of euphoria seized her, and she laughed, sitting all alone in the living room, while the door shook perilously. He had come! Somehow Sean had extricated himself from his engagement to Meg and come after her. She rose and ran to the hall. Her hand was trembling when she finally opened the door.

Sean stood with his closed fist raised, ready to beat the door again. "Why did you shut the door in my face?" he asked with an air of injury.

The old familiar words "What are you doing here?" seemed singularly appropriate, but instead she said breathlessly, "I wasn't expecting you." She studied him minutely for confirmation of her hopes. She expected to see a resolute, take-charge expression, but Sean looked so uncertain that she became unsure herself.

"Who were you expecting? Jeff?" Robyn heard the jealous accents and a smile peeped out. Sean saw her smile and glared. "Or is he already here? Is that the problem?" He made a determined effort to control his fear. It had the effect of making his expression un-readable, impassive.

"I'm alone. Come on in," she said, and walked into the living room. Robyn sat on the sofa. She crossed her legs, one fur-lined slipper bobbing nervously to belie the calm facade she was striving for. Why was he here? The question burned into her, but she was afraid to ask.

Sean still stood up. "Don't stand on ceremony. Have a seat," she suggested.

He threw off his coat and walked woodenly to the chair across from her. Sean was sorry for his outburst at the door and was determined not to lose his cool again. There had been too much of that. This time he meant to do it right. His face was stiff with the effort of behaving decently when every instinct urged him to charge into her bedroom to see if it hid a man. Another side of his mind wanted to pull Robyn into his arms and smother her in kisses.

Robyn wondered about his stiff demeanor. Sean appeared completely unruffled. His hair was neatly combed, and he was freshly shaved. He looked as if he didn't have a nerve in his body. He also looked irre-sistibly handsome. Sean and a tuxedo were made for each other. His lean, athletic grace robbed the suit of its formality and gave it an effortless charm.

"What brings you here, Sean?" she asked to break the tense silence.

"You left rather suddenly last night." His tone made his statement a question.

"I phoned Mom to let her know."

Sean studied her uncertainly. His pride didn't like to confess his eager behavior if she'd already accepted an offer from Jeff. "She told me Jeff wanted to come back early." He looked at her, trying to read her reaction to this. Robyn didn't confirm the lie or deny it, but he could see she was uncomfortable. "So, did you and Jeff have a good trip?" he prodded.

"The weather was quite bad."

"It got worse." He hadn't come plodding through a major snowstorm to discuss driving conditions.

"You don't look any the worse for wear," Robyn said.

"I stopped at a hotel to clean up."

"Not on my account, I hope. You didn't mention what brings you to Syracuse on a Sunday." She leveled a steady stare at Sean. He sat like a rock, but his jaw was quivering, and his eyes were as wary as a shoplifter's.

"What was the big panic that Jeff had to return last night?" he asked, again ignoring her question.

"No panic."

"He just couldn't wait to see you? Is that it?" A flash of blue lightning shot from his eyes.

"Why do you keep asking about Jeff, Sean? And what about Meg? Did she come with you? Surely you didn't abandon her on New Year's Eve. She's at the hotel?"

"Of course not! What would she be doing here?"

"Whither thou goest," she said, and looked for his answer.

The air grew still. They both realized they had reached an impasse. Sean felt his action was self-explanatory. He'd made the first move. Now it was up to Rob to make the next. She understood how their relationship operated.

"Coffee?" she asked with a bright smile.

"Thanks, I could use something to warm me up."

She rose and went to the kitchen, knowing his dark eyes were watching her. She was sorry she hadn't got dressed. A five-year-old housecoat and fleece-lined slippers weren't what she'd have chosen to wear at this crucial moment in her life.

Sean decided it was the formality of the living room that was hampering their progress. The kitchen was a nice cozy place. He got up and followed her.

"Nice apartment."

Robyn directed a disbelieving look at him. The building was the kind of place Sean called tomorrow's slums. "I like the way you've fixed it up," he added to cover his slip.

"It isn't exactly the Rinehart mansion, but it will do," she replied with a fleeting glance to see if this comparison jogged him into meaningful speech. It didn't. She busied herself with cream and sugar. She gave Sean an unhealthy three heaping spoonfuls of sugar.

A soft smile began to defrost his chill as he watched her prepare his coffee. Three years, and she still remembered. If that didn't mean something!

It was when she handed the coffee to him that the tension suddenly became unbearable. Their eyes met over the cup, and the flare of emotion was like lightning striking a tower. Sudden, swift, devastating in its force. How could silence sound so loud? Mute electric reverberations pulsed in the air around them.

Robyn felt the heavy thudding of her heart as their eyes held in a silent gaze. Something important was going to happen. It was that kind of look, that kind of silence. Each waited for the other to break the tension.

If he doesn't tell me he loves me this minute, I'll scream.

Sean saw the desperate hope mirrored in her eyes and was sure he must be imagining it. "I bought the Rinehart house for you, Rob," he said. The words came tumbling out in a rush. "To make up for the one I couldn't afford before."

Sean saw the cup tremble in her shaking hands. He saw the tension ease from her body, and his heart soared. He reached out and set the cup aside. He didn't touch her, but his gaze was a caress, his voice a declaration of love. "Am I too late, darling?"

She stared mutely at him, struck silent by the anxiety in his voice, his eyes. She wanted to register this moment for her personal eternity. It would be an anchor through all the coming years of battling and argument.

She'd only have to remember the love and fear she saw now, and any future doubts would be laid to rest. Whatever foolish things Sean did, it was the depth of his love and his uncertainty of her feelings that were responsible. Just as they had always been. "What about Meg?" she asked.

"It's all over. We had a talk last night." His hands reached for hers. They closed over her fingers in a tight grip. "Meg was just my stupid revenge. It was a rotten thing to do to her. I blame it on temporary insanity when I thought you were marrying Jeff. I had to undo it as decently as possible."

"But I thought last night . . . I mean, you didn't say anything to her when she came to my hotel room. You left with her. . . ."

"Can't you understand that I wanted to be alone to tell her? It was the least I could do. I thought she might rip me up—or you. You didn't think—" He gave her a quick, disbelieving look.

"I'm sorry. I guess I wasn't thinking too straight. I'd made such a fool of myself—" Sean shook his head in denial. "Yes, I did. My nerves were screaming. I already felt as if I'd been waiting an eternity. That hour was almost more than I could endure. Did Meg take it badly?"

"No, very well. She *did* request that I give you a thump for her, though." He smiled. His eyes crinkled at the ends, and his white teeth gleamed. He drew Robyn into his arms and bent down to rest his forehead against hers, rubbing his nose against hers as Eskimo do. "Where would you like it?" he murmured, as his lips worked their way down her cheek in nibbling kisses.

Her arms closed around him and squeezed tight. "Right here," she whispered, and lifted her lips for his kiss.

The first touching of their lips was an instant of hushed poignancy. It held the promise of ecstasies to come. Sean's arms tightened till she was crushed against the solid mass of his body, locked inexorably to him. A wild, delirious fever raged through her as his lips firmed in demand, and she answered unstintingly.

A sea of sensations swirled around her. She stirred as his hands measured the fullness of her hips, then

pushed aside her housecoat, leaving only a flimsy
nightgown between them. She felt naked when his
hands glided over the smooth silkiness of her gown, up
to cup her breasts in a warm, sure, possessive grip. The
longing ache she had endured for so long began to ebb,
leaving in its place a radiant swell of bliss. Sean was
here, he loved her, and nothing else mattered. The
loneliness was over, and she claimed her prize in
grateful victory.

She knew Sean felt the same. His exploring hands
had to touch her all over, to be sure she was real. One
had left her breast reluctantly and brushed up over her
shoulder, cupping her throat with incredible gentle-
ness. His thumb sought out the point of her pulse beat
and rested there, pressing lightly.

She opened her lips and tasted the engrossing
warmth of his mouth. He drew her tongue in deeply,
stroking it with his in a languorous mating game that
unleashed a furious passion.

Sean's fingers tightened imperceptibly on her
throat. Robyn heard an ecstatic moan echo on the air
and wasn't sure whether it was her own or a duet. She
only knew this scalding love couldn't be denied. Not
by time or distance or temper tantrums. Sean was a
part of her. She was only half a woman without him.

She was very much aware now of being a whole one.
He awoke all her dormant femininity. She wanted to
tell him, but this feeling that consumed her was beyond words, so she just went on kissing him. Her
touch must be her love words. She ran her fingers
through the satiny softness of his hair with loving
thoroughness—then along the rugged curve of his jaw,
feeling the strong bone beneath the flesh. His strok-

ing tongue provided a strong distraction. Her insides had turned to warm mush. If this didn't stop soon...

As if reading her mind, Sean drew back and gazed at her. For a moment they looked at each other in wordless wonder.

Robyn smiled weakly. "I look a mess," she said, and rubbed her cheek against his jacket. "And you're all dressed up. Sean, haven't you been to bed at all? You're still wearing your tux."

"I'll sleep tonight. How could I sleep, knowing my girl was with another man?"

"I wasn't," she said. "I just wanted an excuse to leave town. I was running away again. But this time I thought trying to win you back was hopeless. I told Jeff I couldn't give him a lift."

Sean's arms were around her waist. When she leaned back to look up at him, their hips snuggled intimately.

"I should be giving you hell for that, but I'm too relieved. Then it's all over between you two?"

"There was hardly anything to be over. We were just friends. Jill's the one who turned it into a red-hot romance, to make you jealous."

"I don't know whether to thank the girl or give her a good spanking."

"She's getting too old for a spanking."

"Yeah, and since her stunts worked, we won't be too hard on her."

Robyn picked up the coffee and handed it to Sean. She took her own, and they went into the living room, hand in hand. They sat close together on the sofa, unwilling to forgo touching each other.

There were so many little things she wanted to ask him. "Did you really have my picture in your office?" she asked.

"No, in the bedroom of my apartment." He looked around to see if his likeness graced a table.

"In my bedroom, facedown at the moment," she told him. "I've been trying to work up the courage to put you in the garbage. It's at the top of my list of New Year's resolutions."

"I put you under a pile of sweaters in the bottom drawer the night you rattled me off at the skating rink. The truth hurts."

"Tell me about it." She smiled. "A new list of resolutions is called for, Sean. I resolve to—love you," she said. She wanted to say it and say it again, it felt so good.

Sean drew a sigh of contentment. "Amen to that."

Robyn felt she owed some explanation for her behavior in the hotel room. "About last night, Sean," she said, and looked at him uncertainly. "I had drunk quite a bit of wine, but that's no excuse."

"You don't have to apologize. Let me think love had something to do with it."

"It had a lot to do with it. I was nearly crazy with jealousy and the fear that I'd lost you."

He shook his head in consolation. "How do you think I felt? The woman I've wanted ever since I first laid eyes on you was coming on to me, and I couldn't reciprocate."

"I thought I was losing you again."

"You never lost me, Rob. You're the one who ran away," he reminded her.

"It was partly my fault. But when you put that retraction in the paper..."

"I shouldn't have listened to Ed," he agreed. "I knew you better than he did. I felt guilty for not taking the job with Britten. The money was a lot better, and it was a sure thing. I took a chance, going it on my own."

"Oh, but you succeeded! You were right, Sean," she assured him.

"Let's say I was lucky."

They exchanged a look and laughed. This grabbing of the blame to avoid an argument was new to them both.

"That's one fight avoided," Sean said. "We wouldn't argue if we didn't care so much, you know."

"And if we weren't so insecure."

His eyes studied her admiringly. "You're worlds too good for me. How could I not be insecure?"

"Oh, Sean, what have I ever done, compared to you? You're the one who's made his own career out of talent and hard work." She watched as a small smile of pleasure lifted his lips. "Just give me back my engagement ring—my emerald-and-diamond band—and you won't have to worry about being insecure. I'm glad you didn't give it to Meg."

"I bought the big diamond for you, too, to go with the house. It's miles too big for Meg."

"I want my old ring. And my old fiancé. Now, what were you saying about an early wedding?"

*   *   *   *   *

Silhouette Romance

COMING NEXT MONTH

#568 JACINTH—Laurey Bright
Lovely Jacinth Norwood wouldn't let a man inside her secret world, but Mark Harding knew he belonged there. His passion for her was growing—could it melt her icy shell?

#569 THE TAKEOVER MAN—Frances Lloyd
When she bumped into the new director of promotion, advertising executive Kate Camilleri thought she'd never met a more infuriating man—or a more handsome one. Nick Wedderburn's charm might burn her in the end, but Kate didn't care—he could set her heart on fire....

#570 A HALF-DOZEN REASONS—Darlene Patten
Grant Russell was what Karen Wagner had always wanted—affectionate, funny and powerfully attractive. But he was the father of six children! Karen had never seen herself as Maria von Trapp, but she'd climb every mountain to find her dream with Grant.

#571 SOMEDAY MY LOVE—Patti Beckman
When Dak Roberts left town to become an Olympic star, he vowed he'd return to Kathy Ayers someday. That day had come—Dak looked at Kathy and knew, for the first time in his life, he was really home....

#572 POPCORN AND KISSES—Kasey Michaels
Theater manager Sharon Wheeler loved the romance of the old drive-in, but Zachary St. Clair, head of the corporation, thought she was living in the past. He was profits and losses while she was popcorn and kisses. Would the future bring them together?

#573 BABY MAKES THREE—Sharon De Vita
What could be better than a man who'd won a Mother of the Year award? Maggie Magee had never thought about it—until she met ''Wild Bill'' Cody and his little son, Bobby. Now Maggie wanted to win the greatest prize of all—Cody's heart.

AVAILABLE THIS MONTH:

#562 IF YOU LOVE ME
Joan Smith

#563 SOMETHING GOOD
Brenda Trent

#564 THE SWEETHEART WALTZ
Susan Kalmes

#565 THE MAN OF HER DREAMS
Glenda Sands

#566 RETURN TO RAINDANCE
Phyllis Halldorson

#567 SOME KIND OF WONDERFUL
Debbie Macomber

ATTRACTIVE, SPACE SAVING BOOK RACK

Display your most prized novels on this handsome and sturdy book rack. The hand-rubbed walnut finish will blend into your library decor with quiet elegance, providing a practical organizer for your favorite hard-or soft-covered books.

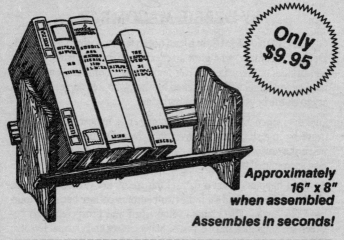

Only $9.95

Approximately 16" x 8" when assembled

Assembles in seconds!

To order, rush your name, address and zip code, along with a check or money order for $10.70* ($9.95 plus 75¢ postage and handling) payable to *Silhouette Books.*

Silhouette Books
Book Rack Offer
901 Fuhrmann Blvd.
P.O. Box 1396
Buffalo, NY 14269-1396

Offer not available in Canada.

BKR-2A

*New York and Iowa residents add appropriate sales tax.

Silhouette Romance™

Legendary Lovers Trilogy

BY DEBBIE MACOMBER....

ONCE UPON A TIME, in a land not so far away, there lived a girl, Debbie Macomber, who grew up dreaming of castles, white knights and princes on fiery steeds. Her family was an ordinary one with a mother and father and one wicked brother, who sold copies of her diary to all the boys in her junior high class.

One day, when Debbie was only nineteen, a handsome electrician drove by in a shiny black convertible. Now Debbie knew a prince when she saw one, and before long they lived in a two-bedroom cottage surrounded by a white picket fence.

As often happens when a damsel fair meets her prince charming, children followed, and soon the two-bedroom cottage became a four-bedroom castle. The kingdom flourished and prospered, and between soccer games and car pools, ballet classes and clarinet lessons, Debbie thought about love and enchantment and the magic of romance.

One day Debbie said, "What this country needs is a good fairy tale." She remembered how well her diary had sold and she dreamed again of castles, white knights and princes on fiery steeds. And so the stories of Cinderella, Beauty and the Beast, and Snow White were reborn....

Look for Debbie Macomber's *Legendary Lovers* trilogy from Silhouette Romance: *Cindy and the Prince* (January, 1988); *Some Kind of Wonderful* (March, 1988); *Almost Paradise* (May, 1988). Don't miss them!

SRT-1